"Jealous? Don't be ridiculous!"

Sara's voice came out high-pitched and breathy. She jerked her face away.

"Ridiculous?" Matt challenged, catching her chin again.

"Yes! Of all the insufferably arrogant ideas—"

"You didn't mind seeing Lydia kiss me good-bye?"

"Why should I mind?" The faint lime scent of his after shave was in her nostrils along with the muskier, more basic smell of his skin. "What possible reason—"

"Well, for one thing, I'd be jealous if I came back to the apartment and found a man doing this to you..."

"This" was a kiss of dizzying, devastating thoroughness. Matt began by brushing his mouth over hers in a teasing, tantalizing movement. After a moment Sara felt the quick, sweet stroke of his tongue. Her breath seemed to catch at the top of her throat. Her body began to respond even as her mind sent out frantic calls for resistance...

Other Second Chance at Love books by
Carole Buck

ENCORE #219

Carole Buck *is a TV network movie reviewer
and news writer who describes herself as a
"hopeful romantic." She is single and currently
lives in Atlanta. Her interests include the bal-
let, Alfred Hitchcock movies, and cooking. She
has traveled a great deal in the United States,
loves the city of London, refuses to learn to drive,
and collects frogs.*

Dear Reader:

February is a good month for romance — not only because Valentine's Day falls on the fourteenth, but also because in so much of the country, freezing temperatures and snowy blasts make you want to snuggle up with someone you love. And when you're not curling close, you can read SECOND CHANCE AT LOVE romances! They, too, are guaranteed to keep you toasty warm and wonderfully satisfied.

We begin the month with *Notorious* (#244) by Karen Keast. Many of you wrote in to compliment Karen on the superb job she did on her first book, *Suddenly the Magic* (#255, October 1984). In *Notorious* she's written a boldly sensual variation on *The Taming of the Shrew*, except in this case veterinarian Kate Hollister sets out to domesticate decadent playboy photographer Drew Cambridge — once she realizes she can't resist him, that is! You'll love watching Kate transform this devil-may-care womanizer into a perfect lover . . . and husband!

Have you ever wondered how magicians bend keys and saw people in half? These intriguing secrets — and more! — are revealed in Lee Williams's most original, riveting romance yet — *Under His Spell* (#245). A phony psychic, a sleek, slobbering leopard, and sexy, black-garbed magician Julian Sharpe make *Under His Spell* an unforgettable romance with a *very* magic touch.

We were pleased and impressed with Carole Buck's first romance for us, *Encore* (#219, September 1984). Now *Intruder's Kiss* (#246) establishes her as one of our brightest talents. I love the opening: Sara Edwards, armed with a squash racquet, is about to tackle two noisy intruders — who turn out to be a huge sheep dog and charming, devastating Matt Michaels. Although wildly attracted to Matt (not the dog!), Sara begins to wonder: Just who *is* Matt Michaels? You'll be delightfully entertained by this lively, sexy, fun-filled tale.

Few writers capture the sizzling chemistry between a hero and heroine better than Elissa Curry. In *Lady Be Good*

(#247), she creates two truly unique characters: Etiquette columnist Grace Barrett is poised and polished, perfectly coiffed and regally mannered; Luke "the Laser" Lazurnovich is an ex-football player who pretends to be even more uncouth than he really is. To tell how this ill-matched pair comes to realize they're perfect for each other, Elissa combines a delicious sense of humor with the endearing tenderness of an emotionally involving love story.

In her outstanding debut, *Sparring Partners* (#177, February 1984), Lauren Fox immediately established herself as a master of witty dialogue. Now, very much in the Lauren Fox tradition, comes *A Clash of Wills* (#248), which pits calm, controlled stockbroker Carrie Carstairs against outrageous, impulsive, infuriatingly stubborn investor/inventor Harlen Matthews. As you can imagine, they're an explosive combination. *A Clash of Wills* is wonderfully fresh and inventive.

You'll be *Swept Away* by our last February SECOND CHANCE AT LOVE romance, #249 by Jacqueline Topaz. "Cleaning woman" Paula Ward has dusted Tom Clinton's penthouse and is "borrowing" his lavish bathroom to prepare for a date, when the devastating millionaire arrives home — with guests! To save her job, Paula impulsively agrees to pose as Tom's wife — with funny, sad, and, above all, sensuous results . . .

February's SECOND CHANCE AT LOVE romances are sure to chase away your winter blahs. So enjoy them — and keep warm!

With best wishes,

Ellen Edwards

Ellen Edwards, Senior Editor
SECOND CHANCE AT LOVE
The Berkley Publishing Group
200 Madison Avenue
New York, N.Y. 10016

Second Chance at Love

INTRUDER'S KISS

CAROLE BUCK

A
SECOND CHANCE AT LOVE
BOOK

INTRUDER'S KISS

First edition published February 1985

First printing

"Second Chance at Love" and the butterfly emblem are trademarks
belonging to Jove Publications, Inc.

Printed in the United States of America

Second Chance at Love books are published by
The Berkley Publishing Group
200 Madison Avenue, New York, NY 10016

INTRUDER'S KISS

Chapter 1

IT WAS 1:05 A.M. on the second Monday in July and someone was breaking into Sara Lynn Edwards's Upper East Side apartment.

She knew the time because she could see the glowing green readout on the face of her digital bedside clock and she knew someone was breaking in because she could hear him.

Sara's heart was pounding and her mouth had gone dry. She'd just made the unpleasant discovery that there was more than a little truth to the cliché about fear making the hair on the back of one's neck stand on end.

Don't panic, she told herself firmly, her hazel eyes wide against the darkness. *Be very, very calm.*

It was hard to be calm when she realized that the intruder was beyond the breaking-in stage. The intruder was now inside the apartment!

Maybe if I lie here quietly and pretend to be asleep, he'll leave me alone. Sara tried to regulate her breathing.

When she had decided to sublet the apartment from her younger sister at the beginning of the summer, Chrissie had warned her that Manhattan was a dangerous place. She'd had a seemingly inexhaustible supply of stories about people who had fallen prey to the Big Apple's criminal element. Even allowing for Chrissie's tendency toward exaggeration, Sara had gotten the message that New York City definitely was *not* Syracuse.

And now she was going to be murdered in her queen-size bed—or worse. There was a terrible irony to it. *She* was the cautious, responsible one in the family; Chrissie was a careless, free-spirited risk-taker. Yet while Chrissie floated blithely through a thoroughly disorganized and rather reckless lifestyle without a scratch, Sara, the disciplined, dependable cleaner-up of everybody's messes, collected more than her share of emotional bruises.

It occurred to Sara at this point—a bit hysterically and certainly irrelevantly—that her intruder was amazingly *noisy*. Weren't burglars supposed to skulk around on sneakered feet? Wasn't stealth supposed to be one of the major tools of their—er—trade?

To her fear-sharpened ears, it sounded as though the person now moving around the apartment's large entrance foyer was unabashedly clumping over the parquet floor. There was the weirdest clickety-scrabble noise as well, plus what she swore was some kind of panting . . . ?

Maybe the intruder was inexperienced, in which case he was probably as panicky as she was. Or maybe he was a genuine crazy who didn't care whether or not his victims heard him.

Her nerves stretched taut, Sara tried to think through the options open to her. She didn't want to just lie there, but what could she do? There was no phone in the bedroom, so she couldn't summon help that way. A combination of repeated paintings and warping had conspired to leave the windows stuck tightly shut, so she couldn't escape. If she screamed, she'd be at the burglar's mercy long before anyone came to her aid—if anyone ever did. She didn't even have a weapon to defend herself with!

"Dammit, Ding, will you watch it?" a low, vibrantly masculine voice demanded. "I know you hate the dark. I'm trying to find the light!"

Oh, Lord, there were *two* of them!

"Ding!" This was followed by a pungent expression of frustration and the rapid snapping sound of a light switch being turned on and off.

Sara's hands curled into fists as she suddenly recalled that the bulbs in the foyer's overhead lighting fixture had burned out the day before. Although she was normally next to compulsive about attending to such things, she'd put off the task of replacing the bulbs because of the exceptional height of the apartment's ceilings. She'd planned to ask the building maintenance man to help her with the loan of a stepladder.

And now . . . if these obviously deranged individuals were serious about turning on the lights before proceeding with their felonious activities, they'd have to roam around the foyer and the open living room area searching for a working light switch or a lamp. That meant that one of them was bound to—

Crash!

—run into her ten-speed bicycle. Sara had had it out for a late afternoon ride through Central Park and had left it standing in the middle of the foyer on top of a layer of newspaper after she'd finished tinkering with and oiling it.

This is my only chance, Sara decided as her adrenal glands kicked into overdrive. She was done being the passive victim-in-waiting. To judge by the yelp of pained surprise that had followed the crash, one of the intruders was temporarily down. Hopefully, the other was confused by the sudden turn of events. Now was Sara's opportunity to make a run for it.

Looking back later, Sara admitted to herself that there

was no reason—*no possible excuse*—for the utterly foolish thing she did next. True, she was frightened and
angered by the invasion of her apartment, but still . . .

What Sara did next was to jump out of bed, grab the
first potentially lethal object she could lay her hands on—
a squash racquet, as it happened—dash to the bedroom
door, and fling it wide open.

Then, standing there clad only in her sheer cotton
batiste nightgown, she said, "Freeze!"

In the heart-stopping silence that followed, Sara realized what she had just done. *You're about to become
a statistic on a police blotter,* she told herself grimly.
*You're going to end up as a part of someone's actuarial
table.*

"Freeze?" It was the same pleasantly distinctive voice
she had heard before. There was no fear, no threat, in
the repetition, this time as a question, of her command,
only an amused and rather stunned disbelief.

Sara's night vision was keen enough to allow her to
make out what appeared to be a motionless tangle of man
and bicycle on the floor about two yards ahead of her.
The voice was coming from there.

"I—I mean it," she said, praying that she could bluff
her way through somehow. "Don't move. And—and that
goes for your friend, Ding, too—oh!"

Something huge and furry leaped on her. Leaped all
over her, in fact. Sara was so startled, she dropped the
squash racquet with a clatter and stumbled, completely
losing her balance. Her last thought in the split-second
before her head cracked against the wall was that Chrissie
had neglected to warn her that some of New York's
criminals had polar bears for accomplices.

The first thing Sara saw when she came to was the
bluest pair of eyes she had ever seen in her life. Set in
a sun-bronzed, lean-featured face and framed by long
pitch-black lashes, they were the kind of blue eyes a

person could willingly drown in—crystalline and cool.

"Wha—" she began fuzzily, trying to sit up. She gave a groan of misery as her head started to throb sickeningly, and she sank back, eyelids fluttering shut again.

"Easy," the now somewhat familiar male voice said soothingly. "It's okay." Gentle fingers stroked comfortingly over Sara's forehead and brushed a few stray tendrils of her auburn hair.

Okay? She'd been assaulted by some type of creature and knocked out. Now she found herself virtually pinned to the sofa by the creature's partner in crime. Things were far from okay!

She was acutely aware of the way the blue-eyed stranger was leaning over her. She could feel the feather-light fan of his warm breath on her face. One of his hard, jean-clad thighs was pressed intimately along one of her softly curving hips. Even with her eyes closed Sara could sense the coiled-spring physicality of this man.

He touched her again, his faintly callused fingertips tracing the line of her creamy-skinned cheek. Sara flinched, a tremor running through her. The contact stopped abruptly and she thought she heard a quick, angry-sounding intake of breath. After a moment she forced herself to look at him again.

Despite the aching of her abused skull, Sara registered the intruder's raffish appearance in meticulous detail. Beneath his tight, well-worn denim jeans and somewhat grubby white knit T-shirt, his body had an athletic balance and whipcord toughness. He topped six feet by an inch or so.

Sara judged him to be about five or six years older than her own twenty-eight years. His hair was black, wavy, and shaggy to the point of being unkempt. One thick lock of it curled carelessly down over his forehead in a comma of ebony. His features were strongly molded and etched with experience. There was an arrogant strength to the line of his nose and jaw. The cast of his well-shaped mouth was distinctly sensual.

He was deeply tanned, which surprised Sara. There were hints of dissipation or, perhaps, exhaustion on his face, which did not. The beginnings of a beard shadowed his cheeks and chin, underscoring his disreputable air.

"Please—" Sara swallowed convulsively. The blue eyes were fixed on her with the intensity of sapphire lasers. "Don't—"

His features hardened. "I'm not going to hurt you," he told her firmly, speaking with infinite care. "Look, I know this has shaken you up pretty badly and I'm sorry about that. But I thought this place was unoccupied. You scared the hell out of me a few minutes ago."

"I scared you?" Sara managed to get out. For some strange and inexplicable reason, she believed him when he said he wouldn't hurt her. But she still wanted to know what he was doing in her apartment!

"Yes, you did," he returned. "What was that 'freeze' routine? Has your brain gone soft from watching police shows on TV or something? Of all the stupid—"

"Stupid?" she gasped, the green flecks in her hazel eyes flashing with indignation.

"Stupid!" he confirmed flatly. "And the squash racquet you were waving around. What was that meant to be? Good Lord—"

"Just what was I supposed to do?" she asked angrily. "Lie there in bed and let you and your accomplice do whatever it was you were going to do?" She struggled to sit up, ignoring the stunned expression on his face. "And where *is* your partner, anyway? Did he get scared and run off or—ohmilord!"

Looking beyond the man sitting on the couch with her, Sara caught sight of what had to be the hugest, hairiest English sheepdog on the face of the earth. The large gray and white animal was sitting next to the toppled bicycle, its tail swishing gently against the floor.

She moaned, lifting a shaky hand to her forehead.

"Easy, easy," the intruder counseled her softly as he flashed a smile that struck Sara even in her unnerved state as the essence of roguish charm. Who *was* this person?

"That dog—"

"That's Dingbat. He's too dopey to get scared and too lazy to run off. Ding, come over here and apologize to Chrissie."

Sara was so unsettled by the approach of the enormous dog—to her shocked eyes, he looked like a furry, two-toned Volkswagen Beetle—that she didn't pick up on the use of her sister's name. Mesmerized, she watched the animal pad to the couch and lift a friendly paw in greeting. The gesture was accompanied by a loud *woof*. Dingbat then cocked his head, apparently waiting for some sign that his overture had been accepted.

"G-good dog," Sara said weakly. *A sheepdog? A burglar with a sheepdog?*

"Not so good tonight," Dingbat's master said, snapping his fingers sharply. "Down, Ding," he commanded. After another bark the dog obeyed. "He probably thought you wanted to play with him when he jumped on you. He's really perfectly harmless. Ding wouldn't hurt a fly— unless, of course, he sat on it. But then, he'd hurt just about anything if he sat on it." He turned on the grin again. Sara felt a queer flutter of response.

Get a grip on yourself, Sara Edwards! Even if he isn't a robber or a rapist, there's something wrong here!

"Who are you?" she demanded as forcefully as she could. She'd edged herself as far away from him as possible. Unfortunately, that wasn't very far.

"Mathieson Michaels—but call me Matt. I'm Lowell's stepbrother."

"Lowell?" she echoed blankly. Lowell something the third was the man Chrissie had been living with in New York before her move to California. Sara seemed to recall her sister saying he was a man with a blue-blooded lineage that could be traced back to the *Mayflower,* and a gilt-edged family business. How could this blue-eyed, black-haired ruffian possibly be related—even by marriage!—to anyone like that?

"You do know who Lowell is, don't you, Chrissie?" Matt asked in an odd tone, his dark brows coming together.

"Lowell's my—why are you calling me Chrissie?"

He grimaced. "Damn! Amnesia."

"Amnesia?" Her voice went up an octave.

His hands closed protectively over her shoulders. "Look, Chrissie, you've had a crack on the head. You're confused." His tone was reasonable and reassuring. "We'll get you to a doctor—"

Except for the thin, ribbon-threaded straps of her nightgown, Sara's shoulders were naked. The feel of his warm palms cupping her bare flesh shook her. Instinctively, she jerked away.

"Chrissie—"

"I don't have amnesia and I don't need a doctor!" she snapped at him, trying to ignore the sudden and unruly speeding up of her pulse. "Furthermore, my name isn't Chrissie! It's Sara."

"Sara?"

"Sara Lynn Edwards. I'm Chrissie's sister."

Matt regarded her in wordless assessment for several long moments. Despite his scruffy appearance, he gave the impression of shrewd intelligence. Lifting her chin with a trace of defiance, Sara met his disconcertingly direct gaze steadily.

"So where's Chrissie?" he asked eventually.

Sara hesitated. "The—the West Coast," she replied at last. To be specific, her younger sister was in Los Angeles pursuing her moderately successful career in show business.

"Hollywood?" he pinpointed with disturbing accu-

racy. "Lowell said something about her being an actress.
I gather that's why she didn't go with him to Zurich for
the summer."

Sara remained silent. She suspected the real reason
Chrissie hadn't gone with Lowell was that after five
months of living with him, she was bored. Sara had long
since accepted the fact that her younger sister was fickle
and essentially faithless . . . just as their late father had
been.

A faint shadow of sadness flickered across her face.

"Sara, are you all right?"

She blinked, slamming her mental defenses into place
to block the sudden intrusion of unwanted memories.

"I'm fine," she said.

"Are you sure? You look—"

"I look what, Mr. Michaels?" she bit out acidly. "Upset? A little pale perhaps?"

"My name is Matt, Sara."

"And my name is Ms. Edwards, Mr. Michaels! Look,
I'm very sorry I'm not beaming like a beauty pageant
contestant at the moment, but I've had a rough night.
First some weirdo—that's you, by the way—wakes me
up out of a sound sleep by breaking into my apartment.
Then that same weirdo—you again—sics his hairy monster of a dog on me! Forgive me, but I'm just not at my
best after something like that."

"I suppose you think I enjoyed being attacked and
nearly crippled by a killer bike and then threatened by a
squash-racquet-wielding female in a see-through nightgown?" he threw back sarcastically.

"See-through—?" she choked out. Oh, yes, the fabric
of her peach-colored nightgown was thin, but it wasn't—

"Okay, okay. I enjoyed the nightgown part," he
amended outrageously.

"What I have on is *not* see-through!"

"Then how do I know you're a natural redhead?"

"Oh!" Sara's anger over this comment left her momentarily speechless.

"Another thing," Matt continued coolly. "I did not break into this place. I let myself in—quite legally—with these." Shifting slightly, he reached into the back pocket of his jeans and fished out a set of keys. He dangled them smugly in front of Sara's face before putting them back into his pocket. "And, finally, this isn't *your* apartment, sweetheart. It's mine. At least it's mine for the next few months."

"What do you mean *yours?* I sublet this apartment from my sister!" Sara exclaimed, protesting. She was paying an appalling monthly sum for the privilege of renting the place, too. Still, despite the price tag, the sublet had been the ideal temporary solution to her housing problem. "She told me her lease runs until the end of September, and since she was going to Los Angeles and I was moving to Manhattan from Syracuse to take a new job—"

"The lease runs until the end of November, Sara, and it's in my stepbrother Lowell's name. Since he was going to be out of the country and I needed a place to stay, I sublet it."

"But—but Chrissie was living here when he went to Europe! Even after she and Lowell broke up—"

"After the breakup Lowell moved into a hotel suite the family firm maintains at the Plaza. He let Chrissie stay on in the apartment because he knew there'd be a scene if he tried to throw her out. My stepbrother hates scenes. He'd shell out a lot more than the rent on this place to avoid one. Besides, he's a gentleman." There was mockery in the way Matt said the last word.

Sara gnawed her lower lip, trying to collect her thoughts. The dull ache in her temples did not help her concentration. She felt as though someone had been pounding on her skull with a tire iron.

"Let me get this straight," she said slowly. "You're

saying that my sister had no right to sublet this apartment to me?"

"You've got it," he confirmed cheerfully.

"But why would she do something like..." Sara's voice trailed off.

"Don't ask me. She's your sister. From the little Lowell said about her—and he and I don't exactly exchange intimate confidences—I would have thought this sort of stunt was right in keeping with her general modus operandi."

It was, Sara admitted with a trace of bitterness. Chances were Chrissie had seen this situation as an opportunity to make some extra money for herself.

"Well, I don't think your stepbrother had any right to sublet the apartment to you, either," she complained defensively. "Not after he more or less agreed to let Chrissie stay here. Unless—"

"Unless?" he prompted, cocking a dark brow.

"Unless you aren't a gentleman and he thought you'd throw her out for him." Even as she said it, Sara knew she was being unnecessarily provocative. Nonetheless, she compounded the insult by adding just barely audibly, *"You* probably *like* scenes."

To her surprise, Matt threw back his head and laughed.

"I hadn't thought of that," he told her, his blue eyes sparkling like a sunlit sea. "But considering Lowell's opinion of me, you could be right. In all fairness, though, I honestly think he believed Chrissie had packed up and left the apartment when he agreed to sublet to me." He paused, a teasing smile quirking the corners of his mouth. "Tell me, what does your sister look like?"

"What—why?"

"Well... if she looks anything like you, I think I could have gotten used to the idea of sharing an apartment... and so forth... with her."

Sara stiffened, instantly wary of this kind of glib flirtatiousness. She'd been taken in by charm before—first

by that of her philandering father, then by that of the
man she had thought wanted to marry her. She was not
about to be taken in again.

"Chrissie and I don't look at all alike," she said curtly.

In Sara's critical opinion her one claim to beauty was
her eyes. They were large, lushly lashed, and remarkable
for their changeability. Aside from that, she was the
possessor of a head of infuriatingly curly mahogany-red
hair, a set of reasonably symmetrical features, and a body
of slightly above-average height that was more boyish
than buxom.

Chrissie, on the other hand, was a statuesque green-
eyed strawberry-blonde.

"Too bad for Chrissie," Matt commented.

"You've never seen my sister," she returned, telling
herself to ignore the implied compliment.

"No, but I've seen you."

Lord, he certainly had all the lines down pat!

"Look," Sara said, regarding him frostily, "That may
work with other women, but it doesn't work with me."
Not anymore, she resolutely added to herself.

"No?" While Sara knew that many men would have
taken her statement as a challenge, there was nothing of
that in his question.

She shook her head gingerly but definitely.

He pulled a resigned, rueful expression. "Too bad for
me," he remarked. He regarded her thoughtfully, his
head tilted slightly.

There was an awkward silence. At least it felt awkward to Sara. Matt seemed perfectly at ease—*at home*,
she thought irritably.

As the pause lengthened, Sara once again became
uncomfortably conscious of his proximity and his dom-
inant maleness. The distinctly speculative look in his
deep blue eyes brought back his previous comments about
the transparency of what she was wearing. Embarrassment—it had to be that!—caused a sudden tautening in

her small breasts. She could feel the stiffening of her nipples against her nightgown.

Even Gary hadn't had this kind of physical effect on her. And she'd been in love with him...

With considerable force of will she kept herself from bringing her arms up in front of her. She was so vulnerable! After working so hard to get back in control of her life, the feeling angered Sara.

She took a deep, steadying breath. "You know," she said critically, "even if you thought this apartment was unoccupied, you might at least have had the decency to call and make certain before you came barging in in the middle of the night."

"Leaving the question of my decency aside, just how was I supposed to do that?" he countered. "For your information, I *did* ring the number I had for Lowell's apartment, but I got a recorded message saying it had been disconnected. I assumed Chrissie must have taken care of that before she split."

"Oh." Actually, Chrissie hadn't bothered. In typical fashion she'd left Manhattan for Los Angeles without paying her final phone bill. In equally typical fashion Sara had settled the account for her. She had then had the old number disconnected and gotten a new listing for herself. "Well, you could have *knocked.*"

"I'm sure you would have appreciated that at one o'clock in the morning."

"I would have appreciated it more than what you did."

"Ummm—but would you have let me in if I'd knocked and asked nicely?"

Sara grimaced, massaging her right temple. "Probably not—no," she replied bluntly.

"Definitely not," Matt amended. He gave her another one of his flashing, freebooter's smiles. "Poor Sara. Come here and let me rub your aching head."

She stiffened as though he'd made an obscene suggestion. "No!"

"I've got magic fingers."

"I'll just bet."

"It's the least I can do."

Her wide hazel eyes glinted green. Sara didn't know whether to laugh or cry or throw up her hands in resignation. She was exhausted, her head hurt, and it was dawning on her with disastrous clarity that what she had envisioned as an orderly transition to a new life had been quite thoroughly disrupted by her sister's thoughtlessness . . . and Mathieson Michaels's sudden appearance.

Oh, well . . .

Sighing, Sara shifted around. Her head drooped forward like a delicate auburn blossom on a slender stem.

"Good girl," Matt commended her, beginning to knead at the tension in the back of her neck.

"A-actually," Sara said after a moment, "the least you can do is leave."

She heard him chuckle. "Always the gracious hostess, aren't you?"

"I reached the limits of my graciousness some time ago."

"And you'd like me to throw myself and my dog out of my own apartment, hmmm?"

Dingbat, apparently curious about the activity on the sofa, got up at this point and ambled over. After sniffing the air for a second he began to nuzzle experimentally at the cushions. Concerned that this might be a prelude to another round of "play time," Sara reached out a tentative hand and petted him lightly. The sheepdog promptly gave her a friendly lick.

"You don't have to throw your dog out," she decided, trying to control the curious little shudders that were running through her. Matt had worked his way up her neck and was now exerting firm but gentle pressure on the area behind her ears. "Ah—he seems trustworthy."

The animal woofed happily.

"Thanks a bunch, Ding. Tell me, Sara, if I jumped

you and cracked your head against a wall, would you consider me trustworthy?"

Sara couldn't see his face, but she didn't trust the silken inquiry in his voice. She could imagine the diabolical gleam that must be dancing in his sapphire eyes. Damn the man!

"Mr. Michaels—"

"Don't tense up on me again. It was only a rhetorical question, Ms. Edwards. In my case, I'm too tired to jump you—"

"You're too—!"

"Besides, I think I came close to emasculating myself on that damn bicycle of yours."

"Close only counts in horseshoes," Sara informed him tartly.

"Nasty, nasty," he reproved her mildly, massaging the base of her skull with a slow, steady circular movement of his thumbs. "So, okay, let me get this straight. The dog can stay, but I get tossed out in the cold, right?"

There was no doubt about it; the ache in her head was easing under his careful ministrations. Maybe he did have magic fingers.

"Mmmm...it's the middle of July. You don't have to worry about the cold."

"Oh, that's really reassuring," Matt retorted. "And to think, your head says you have the capacity for a great generosity of spirit."

"What?"

"Haven't you ever heard of phrenology?"

"Phrenology?"

"That's right. The arcane art of reading the bumps on a person's skull. I probably should have warned you before, but having had your delicate red-haired head in my hands for the last five minutes or so, I now know your most intimate secrets. For instance, this thing here—"

"Ouch!" Wincing, Sara pulled away from him and

shifted back around. "That's not a bump! It's a lump from where I hit my head!" Warning him off with a sharp look, she felt the spot gingerly.

"Sorry," Matt apologized. "You know, I think you should see a doctor—"

"No, I'm all right." Sara shook her head stubbornly. She made a face. "Skull reading! How many women have fallen for that scam?"

"How would a nice girl like you know anything about scams?"

Sara thought about Chrissie...and about Gary. She veiled the suddenly hurt-clouded depths of her hazel eyes with her lashes.

"You'd be surprised," she replied after a moment, striving for a lightly mocking tone.

There was a brief pause. Squaring her slim shoulders in an unconscious assertion of determination, Sara looked at Matt. She saw a disconcerting intensity in the steady cobalt gaze that met her gray-green eyes.

"I think I might be at that," Matt said quietly.

Something—Sara had absolutely no idea what—in the way he said it made her shift self-consciously. She swallowed and inched farther away. You're tired and confused, she told herself. That's why you're reacting this way.

She moistened her lips with the tip of her tongue. "Look, Matt—" she began.

He held up one hand. Some errant portion of her brain noted the sculpted power of his palm and the lean strength of his fingers. She shut her mind to the memory of the soothing yet disturbing touch of those fingers.

"Sara, it's very late," he said. "We aren't going to accomplish anything at this point. Why don't we both get a few well-deserved hours sleep and talk about our situation in the morning? Things may not look any rosier then, but at least we won't be seeing them through bleary eyes."

The mere mention of the lateness of the hour made Sara want to yawn. She had to admit that there was more than a little merit to his suggestion. But she wasn't quite ready to accept it.

"Just *where* did you plan on getting these well-deserved hours of sleep?" she inquired warily.

"Well, since possession is nine-tenths of the law, and you're evidently occupying the master bedroom, I guess I'm stuck with the couch. Or I could throw a sheet over Ding and use him as a mattress."

Sara twisted a stray lock of auburn hair around one finger. "Couldn't you use that suite at the Plaza you mentioned? The one that belongs to the family firm?"

He gave her a brief and quirkily ironic smile. "To tell the truth, I'd probably be less welcome there than I seem to be here. I'm barely a member of the family and certainly not a member of the firm."

"I see," she said, far from sure that she actually did. "I'm not—ah—that is—"

The smile broadened into a mocking grin. "I know, I know. You don't trust me."

"No, it's not that—"

"You do trust me?" His dark brows went up in sardonic disbelief.

"Well..."

"Look, Sara, what do you want? Will it make you feel any better if I tell you I used to be a Boy Scout?"

"You were once a Boy Scout?" She didn't even try to hide her skepticism.

"No. But I'm willing to lie about it if it will help," he declared with calm audacity. "I'll even try to fake a recitation of the Boy Scout oath. What is it—something about being clean, prepared, and kind to small animals?"

She couldn't help smiling. "Never mind. And no, it won't help if you tell me you used to be a Girl Scout, either."

"I was a charter member of the Junior Birdman Secret

Society back when I was a kid," he offered.

"Very reassuring."

"Reassuring enough so you'll let me stay?" He raked a careless hand back through his shaggy night-dark hair. The movement pulled the white knit of his shirt taut, clearly hinting at the lean muscularity of his torso. The three-button closing at his collar was undone, revealing a triangle of tanned chest and dark hair.

Sara looked down, swiping at a nonexistent wrinkle in her nightgown. She was so *aware* of him . . . he evoked such strange, contradictory feelings within her.

"It *is* your apartment," she commented with wry resignation, glancing up at him.

"There is that," he agreed with an obviously assumed air of thoughtful gravity.

Sara sighed. "Well, there's a studio couch in the spare room. I don't know how comfortable it is."

"Probably a hell of a lot more comfortable than some of the places I've slept in my time," he responded with a shrug. After a moment he stretched, fluidly controlled yet restless as a caged cat.

The implications of this remark did not do much for Sara's serenity. Nonethess, she had made up her mind and she would stick to her decision.

"Ah—if you'll let me by"—she made a half-hearted attempt to rise—"I'll get you some linens," she finished in neutral tones.

"No need. Dingbat and I are used to shifting for ourselves."

That she could believe. There was an air of independence—of adventurous competence—about him. Even if Mathieson Michaels hadn't been a Boy Scout, Sara was willing to bet he was prepared for virtually any contingency.

"All right," she said. "But I'd still like you to move back out of the way, so I can get up."

He did so in one smooth effort, then extended a helping hand which Sara pointedly ignored as she got to her feet. Her initial estimate of his height had been accurate: he was a bit over six feet tall. Every inch of those six feet was emphatically and insistently male.

Sara lifted her chin slightly. "I have to go to work in a few hours," she said in a polite, hostesslike voice. "I'll try not to wake you up."

"Just watch out for the bicycle," he counselled her.

"Don't worry about me." She moved by him gracefully and picked up the bike. She wheeled it out of the way and propped it against one of the foyer walls.

"It's trained only to attack strangers, hmmm?" he asked whimsically.

"That's right," she agreed with a sudden sparkle. "And it's better than a Doberman because I don't have to feed it." She glanced around as something occurred to her. "Don't you have a suitcase or something?"

Matt thumbed toward a battered piece of canvas and leather luggage sitting by the door to the apartment. "I've got the essentials in there. Most of my worldly goods are packed in my car. That's parked in an all-night garage a few blocks from here."

"Oh. Well, that's the door to the room you can use for the night." She pointed. "The bathroom is next to it. You'll find fresh towels and sheets in the linen cupboard. If you want—"

"I'm sure I'll be fine." He cut her off with an easy and appealing smile.

"All right," Sara returned with a small shrug. Fighting back a yawn, she crossed to the door of her bedroom. She bent down to retrieve the squash racquet she had dropped during her initial encounter with Dingbat. Lord, had she really done something as harebrained as trying to intimidate an unknown intruder with nothing more than an order to "freeze" and a piece of athletic equipment? "Ummm . . . good night, Mr.—Matt."

"Good night and sweet dreams."

Chapter 2

TAPPING HER GOLD Mark Cross pen against the edge of her desk in an uncharacteristically nervous fashion, Sara finished reading the latest collection of memoranda from the Financial Accounting Standards Board. She neatly checked her name off on the routing list, then placed the thick sheaf of documents on top of the latest issue of the *Journal of Accountancy* in her Out basket.

Chrissie—perpetually overdrawn and overextended—was fond of twitting her older sister about her profession. "The bottom line is boring," she drawled. "Sensible Sara the CPA" was another one of her favorite jibes.

Sara ignored the digs. She was good at what she did and she intended to get better. In addition to keeping up with the latest literature in the field, she was planning to begin taking night courses toward an MBA degree in the fall.

Clicking her tongue, Sara picked up the copy of *The*

New York Times she had purchased at the subway news-
stand on her way to work. It was folded back at the
classified ads. She'd already made a cursory study of the
day's apartment listings, noting several possibilities. At
least they were possibilities on paper. Sara had enough
urban savvy to know that in the Big Apple any apartment
larger than a broom closet was automatically described
as "roomy." A top-floor efficiency unit with a gaping
hole in the ceiling was likely to be written up as an "airy
pied-à-terre with a unique skylight feature."

Damn Chrissie and her conniving! And damn Mathieson Michaels for good measure! Sara had been counting on the sublet to give her time to shop around for a
decent, safe place to live. Now, thanks to last night's
turn of events, she probably was going to have to settle
for something the size of a breadbox at a thousand dollars
a month plus deposit and utilities!

She fought down a yawn. She'd gotten out of bed just
about six hours before, at six-thirty. Normally, she greeted
the day with the disciplined verve of the hostess of an
early morning news show. This particular morning she'd
come very close to slapping off the soft but aggravating
buzz of her alarm and going back to sleep.

Her highly developed sense of responsibility had dis-
suaded her from that course of action. Bleary-eyed and
grumpy, she'd gotten up, showered, applied a discreet
amount of makeup, and ruthlessly brushed her mahogany
curls into glossy order. She'd then donned a trim, crisply
tailored dress-for-corporate-success suit of beige linen
and a simply styled blouse of coral silk. Gold knot earrings, brown pumps and a matching attaché case, and a
brief mist of cologne completed her outfit.

She checked on Matt before leaving. He'd been
soundly, infuriatingly asleep on the studio couch in the
spare room with Dingbat sprawled peacefully on the
floor a foot away. The bedclothes had been bunched
up around him as though he had spent a restless night,

and only a chance draping of the sheets had saved Sara from discovering whether he wore absolutely nothing— or merely very little—to bed.

"As if I cared," she muttered to herself, drawing a lopsided circle around one apartment listing. Sara had seen naked men—all right, *a* naked man—before. She was a reasonably sophisticated twenty-eight-year-old career woman, for heaven's sake, not an inexperienced teenager!

Sara glanced at her wristwatch. Half-past twelve. The only thing on her calendar for the afternoon was a three o'clock meeting. Perhaps she could stretch her lunch hour a bit and check out one or two apartments...

Taking out the small zippered cosmetics case she kept in the bottom drawer of her well-organized desk, Sara did a quick touchup of her makeup. An application of pressed powder banished a hint of shine from her high, smooth forehead and masked the cinnamon-light dusting of freckles on the bridge of her nose. She renewed the subtle smudge of muted gray-green shadow that enhanced her eyes and finished off with a sheer gloss of coral lip color.

Her interoffice line rang.

"Ms. Edwards?" Was it Sara's imagination, or was there a trace of animation—excitement, even—in the receptionist's normally deadpan delivery? "Mr. Math— a Mr. Michaels is here to see you."

Sara had a sudden vision of a blue-jeaned shaggy-haired Matt Michaels standing in the firm's pristinely elegant reception area. Oh, Lord, what if he'd brought that monster of a dog with him?

"Ms. Edwards?" The woman sounded positively breathless!

"Ah—thank you very much, Doris. Tell Mr. Michaels I'll be right out." What was he doing here?

The tall, dark, and undeniably handsome man who came forward to meet her as she entered the reception area was dressed in a navy double-breasted business suit, a pale blue shirt with contrasting white collar and French cuffs, and a blue, silver, and burgundy striped silk tie. He was clean-shaven, and while his thick dark hair still needed cutting, it was neatly brushed back, accentuating the arrogant strength of his lean features. Sara stopped dead in her tracks, staring.

"What happened to you?" she blurted out. Somehow the raffish intruder of the night before had been transformed into a candidate for the cover of *GQ* magazine. While Sara was a firm believer in the restorative powers of sleep, this was a bit much.

"Sara." His tone was suave and his blue eyes reflected his amusement as he took her hands. "You really should have woken me up before you left. We have so much to discuss after last night."

Before Sara realized his intention, he bent his dark head and kissed her full on the mouth. The sensual search of his lips over hers lasted only a moment, but the teasing, testing caress left her trembling inside.

If he hadn't retained his grip on her hands when he broke the kiss, Sara would have slapped him.

"What—what are you doing here?" she said through gritted teeth, her glare telegraphing that if looks could kill, he'd be dead ten times over. She was bitterly aware that Doris, the receptionist, was eavesdropping with unabashed and unprecedented interest. "How did you find me?"

"You left your office phone number on the refrigerator. So I just called up and learned where you were located . . ."

She grimaced in exasperation. "Well—I thought you might need to call me. I didn't expect you to just show up!"

"I haven't just shown up. I'm here to take you to lunch."

Sara could have sworn Doris gave a blissful sigh at that point.

"I'm not having lunch today. I'm going out to look for a new apartment." She jerked her hands free of his and took a step back. He was still close enough so she could smell the crisp, faintly citrusy fragrance of his after shave.

"I've barely moved in and you're moving out?"

"Mr. Michaels!" Sara hissed.

"Ms. Edwards," he countered with a calm smile. "I know I have only one brief nocturnal encounter to go by—"

"Doris, I'm going to lunch now," Sara cut him off in an icily determined voice. She brushed by him and stalked toward the elevators.

"I'm going to lunch, too, Miss Cartwright," Matt told the receptionist with a rakish grin. "It was a pleasure meeting you."

Sara fumed wordlessly as they stood, less than a foot apart, waiting for the elevator to arrive. When it came, jammed full of the predictable noontime crowd, she stepped in and seethed silently as they descended to the main floor. Once they got into the lobby, however, she exploded.

"You have got some nerve! How dare you!"

"How dare I what? Invite you to lunch?"

"Don't give me that injured-innocent routine. Talking about my waking you up this morning—about 'brief nocturnal encounters'—my God! And the receptionist was sitting there lapping it up like a hungry tipster from some tabloid. I have to work with that woman! I'm trying to establish a professional reputation in a new job, you know. This little stunt isn't going to help much."

"Would you have preferred it if I'd mentioned your see-through nightgown and the squash racquet?"

She took a deep breath, struggling for control. "Actually, I would have preferred it if you'd broken your neck last night when you tripped over my bicycle."

"Tough lady, aren't you," he observed with a mixture of admiration and mockery.

"When I have to be," she snapped. And she'd had to be more often than she liked.

He picked up on the undercurrent with unexpected perceptivity, his expression growing thoughtful. "Sara, look, I probably did get a bit carried away with the double entendres upstairs. I'm sorry if I offended you. But, to be perfectly frank, I don't think anyone in your firm—including your receptionist—is going to be shocked or surprised that a beautiful woman like you has an occasional overnight guest or a live-in lover."

"I do not have a lover!" she protested heatedly, then flushed with mortification. *So much for establishing a professional reputation,* she berated herself. *Why not yell out another one of your most intimate secrets in the lobby of the building where you work?*

Somehow she summoned the courage to meet Matt's eyes. What she saw there surprised her. Instead of the ridicule she expected, his compelling gaze held a positive assessment of her. The intensity of it was as unnerving as it was warming.

How long they stood there, Sara had no idea. Matt was the one to finally break the spell, a devilish sparkle of amusement appearing in his expression as he reached forward and traced a feather-light path down her cheek.

"No lover, hmmm? Are certified public accountants required to take a vow of chastity?"

Under normal circumstances Sara would have taken umbrage at such an outrageous question. These were not normal circumstances, however, and instead of finding the inquiry offensive, she discovered it struck her as funny—and weirdly flattering. After all, Matt *had* called her beautiful, hadn't he?

She gave a helpless gurgle of laughter. "If you check the fine print in the AICPA's set of GAAPs, I'm sure you'll find a chastity clause," she assured him. I must be suffering some delayed reaction from that crack on the head last night, she decided. Sensible Sara has a scrambled brain.

"Would you mind translating the alphabet soup?"

"Not at all." She cleared her throat. "The AICPA is the American Institute of Certified Public Accountants."

"And GAAPs?"

"Generally accepted accounting principles."

"I see." He quirked a brow. "Chastity clauses aside, is there anything in the GAAPs that prohibits you from coming to lunch with me?"

"Do you have somewhere particular in mind?"

"I'd just as soon avoid the three-martini-lunch bunch, if you don't mind. And until I'm sure of your temper, I think I'd be smart to opt for a place with nothing but blunt eating utensils."

"You find something threatening about the idea of me with a steak knife in my hand?"

"Lady, you scared me witless armed with nothing more than a squash racquet."

"I wish you'd forget about that!"

"No way, Sara. Come on, let's find someplace to eat."

They ended up at a pleasantly uncrowded French restaurant about three blocks away from the Madison Avenue building that housed the accounting firm for which Sara worked.

"Would you like some wine?" Matt asked after they'd ordered.

Sara shook her head. "No, thank you. If I drink wine in the afternoon, I get sleepy." She took a sip of ice water. "And if I drink it at night, I get silly."

"I'll have to file that away for future reference."

"Don't clutter up your mind with information you're

never going to have a chance to use," she advised with a smile.

"My motto is Be Prepared."

"That's the Boy Scout motto. And you've already told me you never belonged to that particular organization."

"True," he conceded. "But I still like to be prepared."

"So do I." Sara took a piece of crusty French bread from the wicker basket in front of her. "You know," she reflected, "I really should be spending this lunch hour looking for an apartment."

"What's wrong with the one you have now?"

She gave him a cool look. "Aside from the fact that it's not mine and you're living there, it's a terrific place."

"Ummm—then why move out?"

Sara fingered her silverware. "Matt, if you're leading up to a proposition, I think I should warn you that there are several knives on the table."

"Not a proposition, Sara. A . . . business proposal."

Reaching into his jacket, he withdrew a manila envelope. He tossed it down on the table.

"What—?"

"It's a lease. Lowell's subletting to me. I'm willing to sublet to you on a fifty-fifty basis for the rest of the summer." He grinned across at her. "We could be roomies."

"We're total strangers!"

"We've already spent one night together," he reminded her. "Ah—thank you."

The arrival of the waiter forestalled Sara's instinctive retort. Plastering a polite smile on her face, she waited silently as the man served their lunch with deft, economical movements. There was a mushroom omelette for her and a parsley-spangled fresh seafood salad for Matt.

"I hope you enjoy your meal," the waiter said with a precise nod before moving away.

"Will you stop saying things like that?" Sara demanded.

Matt opened his white linen napkin. "You have an aversion to hearing the truth?"

"I have an aversion to hearing the truth the way you tell it. You could probably make a Sunday school picnic sound salacious." She picked up her fork and stabbed at her entree.

"I'm not going to ask which part of my anatomy you're fantasizing about at the moment," Matt commented dryly, drawing a wrathful glare. "Sara, look, this is a very practical suggestion I'm making. If I had anything— er—salacious in mind, I'd say so."

"Oh, really?"

"Yes, really. I'm offering you a contract, not a come-on." He tapped the envelope. "You need a place to stay for a while. I've got one. It's as straightforward as that."

Sara took a bite of the fluffy egg and mushroom dish. Somehow, despite his reasonable tone and respectable appearance, she doubted that anything about Matt Michaels was as "straightforward as that." She reminded herself that some of the worst rogues around wore exquisitely tailored Savile Row suits and hid their true natures behind beguiling masks of charm.

"I don't know anything about you," she protested.

He forked up several nuggets of shrimp and diced celery. "What's to know? I'm thirty-four years old, single, and I've already confessed that I never joined the Boy Scouts. I have it on good authority that I don't snore and I've been told I make a very mean spaghetti sauce. My dog is housebroken and so am I. I'm willing to let you keep the master bedroom if you don't object to my using the living room for an orgy once a week. You're welcome to join in, of course."

"Matt!" She nearly choked on a mouthful of omelette.

"Sara, your sister lived with my stepbrother in that apartment. If we shared the place for the summer, we'd be upholding a family tradition."

"You know, I thought all that nonsense you were

spouting last night—especially that stuff about skull reading—was the the most ridiculous con job I'd ever heard. I was wrong."

"You still don't trust me, hmmm?"

"Is there any reason why I should? Oh, I believe you *are* Lowell's stepbrother and that you *do* have a legal right to the apartment, but other than that—" She rolled her eyes.

"Don't I get a few Brownie points for refraining from ravishing you in your sleep?"

Sara's pulse started to pound. She set down her fork with exaggerated care, frankly appalled by the erotic images that were flashing through her mind in response to his use of the word *ravishing*. She swallowed hard.

"You—you were exhausted, remember?"

He speared a piece of lobster meat and ate it with relish. "Not at four this morning, I wasn't."

"And just what is that supposed to mean?" she asked in a carefully measured voice, trying to ignore the obviously sensual pleasure he was taking in his meal.

"I had trouble getting to sleep," he said finally. "I kept thinking about your passing out from that blow to the head, and I was worried about the possibility of concussion. After tossing and turning I got up and checked on you. You were very appealing lying there, all cuddled up—"

"You came into my bedroom and looked at me?"

"There wasn't much to look at, really. The sheet was pulled all the way up around your neck. Of course, I had a pretty good idea of what you were hiding..." He paused provocatively. "After I made certain you were sleeping normally, I nobly took myself back to my lonely, lumpy bed."

"And just how did you 'make certain' I was—" She broke off abruptly. She didn't want to know. "Don't answer that," she said hastily.

"Okay."

Sara gnawed her inner lip. The thought of him bending over her while she slept sent a shiver running through her again. She was struck by an overwhelming sense of her own vulnerability. And yet... wasn't she being a little hypocritical about the situation?

"Sara?" His voice was soft and velvety.

She picked up her fork again and chased a mushroom cap around her plate. "I looked in on you, too," she admitted after a moment. "Before I left for work."

"I see." Something in his tone made her forget the mushroom. He couldn't have been faking this morning, could he? She could have sworn he was dead to the world! "In that case, you do know *something* about me," he continued.

She cleared her throat. "You mean, that you sleep—ah—"

"In the raw. Yes."

"I didn't notice."

"If you had, do you think it would have influenced your thinking about sharing the apartment?"

Her mouth dropped open. The man was incorrigible! "Are you asking me—"

"If the idea of my sleeping in the buff bothers you, I'm willing to make a few concessions."

"Why are you so eager for me to stay in the apartment?"

"Well, for one thing, I wouldn't have to worry about handling intruders. And you'd probably be useful when it comes time to try to balance my checkbook."

"Be serious!"

To her surprise, he reached across the table and captured one of her hands between his palms.

"Okay, serious. I'm a sucker for independent-minded natural redheads who've gotten the dirty end of the stick through no fault of their own. It's a big apartment, Sara.

There's plenty of room for two—three, if you count Ding. We probably won't run into each other more than once or twice a week."

For some strange reason Sara took no comfort from his last observation. "Well—"

"At least stay until you've found another place to live," he suggested, stroking her wrist with his thumbs.

"But you don't know any more about me than I know about you." She was capitulating even as she continued to object.

"I'm a fast learner."

He was also a very slick operator, Sara decided when she got home shortly after six that evening. She'd canceled her usual Monday squash game at her health club, and was not in the best of moods. It had been a long, trying day, and she was feeling increasingly unsettled about the decision she had made over lunch.

"Stay, Ding!" Matt's voice commanded sharply as she let herself into the apartment. She froze in the doorway as she saw the sheepdog come bounding down the foyer toward her in an enthusiastic show of canine friendship. To her astonishment, the animal stopped about two yards from her and simply woofed out a greeting.

Matt materialized from the kitchen. He was barefoot and had exchanged his business suit for bluejeans and a washed-out red sweat shirt. He had a dishtowel tossed over one shoulder and was holding a head of romaine in his left hand.

"Welcome home," he said.

Keeping a watchful eye on Dingbat, Sara shut the door and deposited her attaché case and squash racquet on the floor. "Ah—hello," she returned. "And hello to you, too, Dingbat."

Evidently taking this as an indication that his obvious affection was reciprocated, the dog padded forward and nuzzled his furry head against Sara's legs. She responded by petting him and scratching around his ears.

"That's enough, Ding," Matt said after a few moments. He snapped his fingers and pointed. "Back into the kitchen."

After giving a final *woof*, Dingbat shambled off as ordered.

"Sorry about that," Matt said easily.

Sara shrugged, unbuttoning her linen jacket. She glanced around curiously. "I see you're both making yourselves at home," she observed. There were several cardboard cartons stacked by the door to the spare room and a pile of what she judged to be dirty laundry dumped next to them.

He smiled. "This is strictly transitional chaos. I've been living out of boxes and suitcases for so long, it's going to take me a day or so to sort everything out."

"You've been traveling?"

"Just . . . moving around a lot."

"Oh." The fractional hesitation in his reply struck Sara as a bit strange, but she wasn't certain how to follow up on it.

"Look," he picked up smoothly. "Why don't you change into something a little more comfortable while I finish up the salad. We can eat anytime you're ready."

Sara blinked. "You've made dinner?"

"I've created a culinary masterpiece," he corrected her, gesturing with the romaine. "Haven't you detected the delicate aroma—"

There *was* something in the air.

"Garlic and oregano," Sara said with assurance.

"My spaghetti sauce."

"This really was delicious," Sara declared about forty-five minutes later. She sighed contentedly, resting her elbows on the top of the butcher-block table in the middle of the kitchen. The pasta—purchased fresh at a nearby gourmet shop—had been cooked to al dente perfection.

The sauce had been spicy, thick, and rich with sweet sausages and mushrooms. A crisp salad completed the meal.

"It's an old Sicilian recipe," Matt told her. He rose and began clearing their plates. When Sara moved to help, he told he to remain where she was.

With a little shrug Sara obeyed. She fished a pale green coin of cucumber out of the teak salad bowl before Matt removed it. Nibbling on it, she watched him carry out a series of domestic chores with unthinking efficiency. Dingbat was lying comfortably by the refrigerator, his large paws resting protectively on either side of a sunshine yellow feeding dish. She smiled as Matt was forced to step over or around the dog for the fourth or fifth time.

"Wouldn't it be easier to ask him to move?" she asked.

"Asking is simple. Getting him to do it is the trick."

With a cheerful disregard for table manners Sara licked a trace of oil and vinegar dressing off her fingers. She felt wonderfully at ease. She'd changed out of her suit into an oversize apple-green T-shirt and white slacks. With her face cleansed of makeup and her auburn hair casually fluffed, she looked like a college student.

"I can see your point," she conceded. "It—it was very nice of you to fix dinner for me."

"For us," he amended, coming back to the table. "I wanted to drive home another of the many advantages of having a roommate."

"Well, I hope you're not counting on me to reciprocate. I'm not much of a cook under the best of circumstances, and after a long day at the office—" She gestured expressively.

"More Chianti?" he asked, reaching for her glass.

Sara brushed his hand away. "I've had enough, thank you," she told him. She felt a spurt of electricity run through her as they touched. I've had more than enough, she thought.

"Are you about to get silly?"

She remembered her comment over lunch. "I'm about to fall asleep."

"You do look tired. Did you have a rough afternoon? Problems with the receptionist?"

"Please!" Although Sara was certain there had been a glint of speculation in Doris Cartwright's beady eyes when she'd returned from lunch, there had been nothing overt. "Doris was fine."

"You're not having some reaction to last night, are you? A headache—dizziness?"

"No. I'm okay. I just didn't get much sleep . . . and it was a long day with the ledger books."

"I thought ledger books went out with green eye-shades."

"True. Nearly everything's computerized now."

He recorked the wine and put the bottle into the refrigerator.

"How did you happen to go into accounting?" he asked, stepping over Ding and moving to the sink.

Sara smothered a small yawn. "I've always been good with numbers," she replied. "My parents had a small business back in Syracuse and I got my first taste of bookkeeping helping them when I was fairly young. Then I started handling the household accounts when I was sixteen or so."

"And why was that?" He sounded genuinely interested.

She twisted a lock of hair around one finger. "My . . . father walked out. For the third and final time. My mother wasn't—isn't—very good at budgeting money or balancing checkbooks. So I took over. She—my mother—is remarried now. My stepfather's a retired pharmacist, and he thinks it's very feminine that she doesn't know a credit from a debit."

"And you think?" he prompted.

"I think it's very foolish. Still, he's a good man and

he loves her. And she seems to love him." She was surprised by her candor. Normally, Sara was very reticent about her background.

"Did you study accounting in college?"

"I took a joint degree in accounting and finance." She smiled. "I suppose that sounds very dull."

"Money matters are seldom dull," he commented dryly.

"No, I suppose not," she agreed. His tone struck her as odd. Her initial impression had been that Matt Michaels didn't care a great deal about money or material possessions. Yet, from his appearance in her office earlier in the day, he was obviously at ease with the more expensive things in life. She shook her head a little, not wanting to dwell on the contradiction at the moment.

"Sara?"

"What?"

"Are you all right?"

"Fine. I—I was just thinking about one of my old college professors. To listen to him, you would have thought accounting was the most exciting profession in the world. He believed CPAs should be the 'watchdogs of corporate integrity.' He was also fond of reminding us that the IRS—not the FBI—finally got Al Capone."

He grinned in appreciation, but the smile didn't reach his eyes. "And how many mobsters—or sticky-fingered executives—have you unmasked with your faithful calculator?"

The question caught her by surprise. Unable to hide the reaction it triggered, she went white.

Only one sticky-fingered executive. Gary Beaumont. The man she trusted, loved, and had wanted to marry.

The phone on the kitchen wall rang. His dark brows drawn together in a frown and his cobalt gaze fixed on her, Matt picked it up.

"Hello? Oh...yes. She's right here." He extended the receiver. "It's your sister."

Sara took a deep breath, composing herself. Forcing

herself to ignore the trembling and hurt inside, she got up from the table, crossed the kitchen, and took the phone.

"Thank you," she said quietly. She put the receiver to her ear. "Hello, Chrissie?"

"Sara? Who is that divinely sexy man who just answered the phone?" Chrissie's throaty voice bubbled from the other end of the line. "He sounds tall, dark, and handsome to me. What's he doing there with you?"

Sara let the implied putdown go. "His name is Mathieson Michaels," she said. "He's Lowell's stepbrother. You do remember Lowell, Chrissie, don't you?"

"Of course I—Lowell's stepbrother? What's happened?"

Sara proceeded to give a concise although somewhat censored version of what had been going on. Chrissie punctuated the account with gasps of indignation and groans of shock.

"Lowell sublet the apartment to his stepbrother?" she exploded as Sara finished her recitation. "That rat! That Brooks Brothers bast—"

"Chrissie!"

"He said I could have the apartment while he was in Zurich!"

Sara leaned against the wall. While her younger sister's view of the world was a self-centered one, this reaction was a bit extreme, even for her.

"Chrissie, he may have said *you* could have the apartment, but I seriously doubt that he intended that you sublet the place to someone else! Especially when he was still paying the rent."

There was a tiny pause, then Chrissie came back strong.

"Well, why shouldn't I have?" she demanded. "You needed a place to stay and I needed some money for L.A. I mean, I can't keep showing up at auditions in the same clothes over and over."

"It was wrong."

"Oh, God, don't get all moralistic on me, Sara. I could kill Lowell, I really could! I was counting on that rent money. I'm up for a part in a commercial, and I need—"

"Chrissie, aren't you even going to ask what I plan to do about this mess you've gotten me into?" Sara interrupted.

There was another pause. "Oh . . . sure. What?"

"I'm going to share the apartment with Matt for the summer. Or until I find a place of my own."

"What?"

Sara repeated her statement, taking an odd satisfaction in having penetrated her sister's bubble of self-absorption.

"You're going to live with a man?"

"That's one way of putting it."

"But you hardly know him!"

"I know he's your ex-lover's stepbrother. He has a dog named Dingbat. And he makes great Sicilian spaghetti sauce."

"He's also some kind of black sheep, Sara."

"I beg your pardon?"

"Oh, I don't know all the details. Lowell mentioned him only once or twice, which was weird, considering the way he droned on about his family all the time. Anyway, I did overhear this one phone call between them."

"And?"

"And they were arguing. I remember because Lowell was always so cool and calm. But he was in a real snit over his call from Mack—"

"Matt."

"Right. Lowell was ranting about the family name and Matt's low-life connections being an embarrassment. I couldn't hear everything, but he mentioned the police and bail money."

Sara's throat tightened. She glanced over toward Matt. He was standing by the sink with his back to her, rinsing dishes. As though feeling her eyes on him, he looked over his shoulder questioningly. Sara managed an unsteady smile.

"You probably misunderstood," she said flatly.

"Mmmm . . . maybe. But, you know, there was something suspicious about his voice when he answered the telephone."

"That's not what you said originally."

"Oh? Oh, the tall, dark, and handsome bit. A man can be divinely sexy and rotten to the core, too, Sara. I think you should reconsider this sharing business."

"Everything's fine."

"After all, you're not the best judge of character when it comes to men, are you?" Chrissie continued thoughtlessly. "Remember Gary?"

"I'd just as soon not, thank you. Look, Chrissie, did you have a reason for calling?" Matt had gone back to his clean-up chores, but Sara sensed he was listening intently to her end of the conversation. She moistened her suddenly dry lips.

There was a long silence from the other end. Maybe Chrissie was lonely out in Los Angeles and had phoned for a sisterly chat? Sara doubted it. Chrissie invariably placed such calls collect. No, her younger sister wanted something, but she was shrewd enough to know this wasn't the time to ask for favors.

"I suppose you want back the rent money you paid me," Chrissie said finally. She sounded as though she was pouting.

Sara sighed wearily. "Never mind the money. I would have had to pay rent to somebody anyway."

"Oh, terrific! Look, I've got to run. I'm meeting a producer for drinks later and I've got to get my nails done. Maybe you should check out this Matt guy a little more, Sara. He may be a hunk and all that, but I warned you about Manhattan men—if they're not trying to rip you off, they're—"

"Thank you, Chrissie," Sara cut in, not wanting to hear any more. "I've got to go, too. Have a nice manicure." She hung up the phone.

"There are some fresh strawberries for dessert if you want them, Sara," Matt said, opening up the dishwasher. His voice was politely conversational and he didn't turn to look at her.

"No, thank you," Sara returned. "I'm not . . . hungry."

Matt didn't argue with her.

Chapter 3

"WELL, SARA, ALL I can say is that the only time somebody broke into *my* apartment, I lost my stereo set, a color television, and my Great-aunt Monica's pearls." Elayne Berman paused to spoon a large dollop of frozen yogurt topped with coconut and raisins into her mouth. "But you, you end up gaining a gorgeous hunk of a roommate who cooks!"

Sara speared a chunk of pineapple out of her fresh fruit salad. "I never said he was gorgeous."

"You didn't say he was Quasimodo, either. Come one. Six feet plus, blue eyes, black hair—that sounds like enough to get a girl's hormones humming. And if he could actually draw a reaction from that terminally indifferent receptionist at your office, he's got to be hot stuff."

"Elayne!"

"I, personally, think it's terrific. You've been here in Manhattan since the end of May, and you haven't gone out once. There is more to life than auditing the Acme Widget Corporation's balance sheet. As I so often remind myself, you've got to use it, or you'll lose it."

Sara shook her head. She was beginning to regret having been quite so frank with Elayne. The two of them had met and become friends in college, and they'd stayed in touch after graduation. Elayne, who was a media buyer for a large advertising agency had welcomed Sara's move to Manhattan with enthusiasm. Just an inch or so over five feet tall and compulsively fond of chocolate, she was constantly fighting the battle of the bulge. One of the first things she had done after Sara's arrival in New York City was to persuade her to take advantage of a two-for-one offer at a popular health club. The two of them met nearly every Monday night for an energetic set of squash and a relaxing round of "girl talk" over one of the low-calorie specials served at the club's restaurant.

"Is your husband aware of this philosophy?" Sara asked. Elayne was married to an editor at a well-known publishing house.

"Blissfully," the other woman replied smugly, her brown eyes gleaming.

"How is Paul, by the way?"

"Oh, no, you don't!" Elayne shook her head, her fashionably permed brown hair bouncing. "No changing the subject. You've been living with this Matt Michaels for a whole week. I want all the delicious details."

"We're sharing an apartment, not living together."

"Picky, picky. Okay, so what does he do?"

Sara toyed with a strawberry. "I'm not certain," she admitted. "To tell the truth, he doesn't seem to do much of anything. He's there when I leave in the morning and he's there when I get back in the evening, and there's no sign he's accomplished anything in between."

"Does he go out at all?"

"He runs early in the morning in Central Park with his dog. And he must go out shopping, because somebody's keeping the larder stocked, and it isn't me. He went out two nights last week and Sunday afternoon, but only for a few hours."

"Maybe he's taking it easy—he's on vacation."

"I don't think so, Elayne. I asked him what he did for a living—I mean, it seemed only fair, considering the fact that he's always questioning me about my work."

"And?"

"And he said he was self-employed."

"Ummm . . ." Elayne stirred her yogurt thoughtfully. "Maybe he's unemployed and sensitive about it," she suggested.

"I wondered about that," Sara said. "But he's got money, Elayne. *Lots* of money."

"Oh?"

"For example, he dresses very casually, but all his clothes are high quality and expensive. His car is one of those hand-crafted imports that accelerates to seventy as soon as you turn on the ignition, and costs more than a small house. He's traveled all over the world—"

"How do you know that?"

"I saw his passport when I was helping him move his things into the spare room. There was this huge envelope full of papers, and the passport fell out of it. It was covered with stamps."

"So?"

"So—I don't know exactly, Elayne. It's just . . . odd somehow. There are things that just don't add up—"

"Thus speaketh the CPA," Elayne quipped.

"No! The other night, for instance we ordered in Chinese food for dinner. You should have seen the wad of bills Matt pulled out to pay the delivery boy!"

"Could be he pulled off a bank heist and is laying low."

Sara knew her friend meant it as a joke, but she couldn't laugh.

"Sara?" Elayne questioned, her pert features melding

into a frown. "Hey, I was just kidding! Good Lord, you don't seriously think that this guy is some kind of . . . of . . ."

"Criminal? No, I don't suppose I seriously think that. But he's just so—so *elusive*." And attractive. And intriguing.

"Well . . . maybe he's just one of the idle rich, did you ever think of that? You said his stepbrother has money. Matt probably does, too."

"He's estranged from his family." A black sheep with low-life connections, Chrissie had said.

"So? Estranged doesn't mean disinherited or disowned. Look, okay, the man has expensive tastes and a mysterious ability to support them. I'm sure there's a logical explanation. I know you're wary of men, Sara, and I can't say that I blame you after your experience with Gary, but I think you're being paranoid. Unless— unless there's something more?"

Sara hesitated. "He's got scars," she said finally.

"Scars?" Elayne's eyebrows went up.

Sara nodded. She had seen them the third morning after Matt moved in. He'd been out for a run with Dingbat and had returned, drenched with perspiration from his exertions and the summer heat. He'd come into the kitchen for a glass of water, stripping off his T-shirt as he did so.

His pleasant greeting and Dingbat's inevitable *woof* had made Sara glance up from her coffee and *Wall Street Journal*. As she did so she got a look at his naked back. Her hello died in a gasp of shock she couldn't quite suppress.

What she saw was a pair of wicked-looking scars cutting a ragged course diagonally across his left shoulder blade, then furrowing downward, running parallel to his spine.

Matt had turned at the sound, the blue of his eyes going as hard as lapis lazuli when he saw her expression.

"My back," he said flatly, his body taut. "Sorry, I

wasn't thinking. It's not a very pretty way to start the day. I'll go put on another shirt."

"No!" Sara had protested, her cheeks growing hot under his steady stare. "I—you can put on a shirt if you want to, of course. But don't do it because of me, please. Your back—I was surprised, that's all."

For some inexplicable reason it had seemed very important to convince him that she wasn't repulsed by what she had seen. True, the scars weren't pleasant to look at, but after the first moment of shock her main impression of them had been of the way they underscored the breadth and supple strength of his back.

Returning her concentration to Elayne, she elaborated. "He has scars on his back."

"Was he in an accident or something?"

"I—I asked him that same question. He shrugged and said 'or something.'" She'd also asked if there was any pain. Matt's answer had been a terse, "Not anymore."

"Hmmm. Well, scars don't prove anything," Elayne declared, helping herself to several grapes from Sara's salad. "A lot of people have scars. My husband has a scar."

"From an appendix operation."

"How do you know that?" The question was mock suspicious.

"You wrote me this incredibly long and graphically detailed letter about Paul after you decided he was the one."

"Oh, yes, I remember."

"You think I'm making a big deal out of nothing with this Matt situation, don't you?"

"We-e-ll, I can understand your being cautious. You did originally mistake him for a would-be rapist or burglar, and they say first impressions die hard. And you've always been very—um—conservative in the way you live. I can see you being thrown by someone who's a bit more—ah—bohemian." Elayne was obviously choosing her words carefully. "And maybe . . . just possibly maybe . . . you're attracted to this guy and you're looking for reasons to steer clear of him."

Sara sighed. She was honest enough to admit to herself that there was some validity to her friend's observation. She was attracted to Matt. Her physical awareness of him had increased, not decreased, during the past seven days. She enjoyed his company, his provocative sense of humor, and his wide-ranging intelligence. There were moments when she felt an almost tangible attunement between them.

And there were other moments when she felt the walls go up . . . whether from her side or his, she couldn't tell. Matt Michaels had secrets to hide.

Sara didn't—couldn't—trust him. To do that would be to invite the hurt, the helplessness, she had sworn never to feel again.

"I suppose I am overly cautious," she said slowly, her hazel eyes cloudy.

"He hasn't tried anything, has he?"

"No." The neck rub that first night and the brief, questioning kiss at her office the next day had been as intimate as they'd gotten. Of course, there *were* moments when his blue eyes ran over her provocatively that suggested he'd like to try something . . . and she'd found her own thoughts colored by an erotic wishfulness as she watched him. But there had been nothing more than that. "No, he hasn't, Elayne."

"Is that relief or regret I'm hearing?"

Sara gave a small laugh. "I don't know."

What happened four days later did absolutely nothing to resolve her mixed feelings.

A brilliantly clear summer day had given way to the welcome cooling of early evening. Sara had bypassed her usual bus trip home in favor of a walk. It was a journey of more than two dozen blocks, but she didn't mind. Buying herself a white paper cup of lemon ice from a street vendor, she strolled in leisurely fashion up Madison Avenue, indulging in a bit of window-shopping along the way. She was looking forward to the weekend.

On impulse, she ducked into a florist's and purchased two large bunches of flowers. One of the things she disliked about Lowell's apartment was its stark high-tech decor. While her own furniture—still in storage in Syracuse—was contemporary in style, it had a comfortable, inviting warmth. She'd picked up a few inexpensive odds and ends since coming to New York City in an effort to soften the trendy austerity of the sublet.

She suspected Matt was no more fond of the decor than she was. Although he kept the spare room in sparkling order, he seemed to enjoy giving the rest of the apartment a lived-in look. He'd brought several boxes of books with him—as eclectic an assortment of reading material as Sara had ever seen—and had sprinkled them haphazardly about the place within days of his arrival. He'd also produced a remarkable collection of folk art from around the world.

There was one particularly striking black lacquered vase from the Orient, which Sara especially liked. She picked out a mix of snow white and ruby red carnations with that in mind.

She was feeling pleasantly tired and a bit warm by the time she reached the apartment building. The cool, air-conditioned atmosphere of the lobby felt lovely. Once inside the elevator Sara pulled off the salmon and jade striped silk scarf she'd used to accessorize her figure-flattering cream knit dress. Sniffing the spicy fragrance of the carnations, she absently undid several of the tiny fabric-covered buttons on the front of her dress.

Stepping out of the elevator, she began fishing around her purse for her keys as she walked down the hall. At the same moment she found them, the door to the apartment swung open.

Matt was standing there, clad in nothing but one of his innumerable pairs of form-fitting jeans, running shoes, and a partially unbuttoned work shirt. Standing next to him, her pink-polished nails resting lightly on his chest as she kissed him, was a woman Sara had never seen before.

She was forty at the very least, and she was stunning in a chic, utterly self-assured way. Her ash-blond hair was styled in a classic chignon and her pampered complexion was lightly tanned and flawlessly made up. She was wearing a pure white linen suit. She was also wearing a wedding ring and a flashing diamond solitaire.

"Sara!" Matt exclaimed.

"I—I didn't realize you were having company," Sara said inanely, trying not to stare.

"Not company," the blond woman corrected her. "Strictly business." She gave Matt a coolly amused smile.

"Bus—?" Sara began, suddenly feeling a little sick. Matt and a married woman doing "business" together?

"Sara, this is Lydia Follett," Matt jumped in smoothly. A little *too* smoothly, Sara thought. "Lydia, Sara Edwards."

Lydia nodded. Sara murmured a polite hello. After a moment the blonde looked at the wafer-thin platinum watch on her left wrist. She raised one of her delicately penciled eyebrows.

"Six-thirty," she commented. "I hadn't expected our little session to run quite so long, Matt."

"We both got carried away," he replied, giving Lydia one of his most rakish smiles. There was an intimacy—an understanding—between them. Sara could feel it . . . see it.

"Hmmm. Well, I admit it was tantalizing, but I'm far from satisfied."

"You never are, Lydia. You're insatiable."

"I'm not the only one. Incidentally, I've given your name to someone—"

"I've got more than enough work now."

"Just listen to her proposition, darling. She wants to pay you a lot of money to do what you like best." She patted her hair complacently. "So nice to have met you, Miss Edwards."

"It was nice to have met you, too."

"I'll call you next week, Matt."

"Fine. Let me walk you to the elevator. Sara, I'll be back in a minute. Ding's shut up in your room. I hope you don't mind."

Why should I mind? Sara asked herself irritably as she slammed into the kitchen and dropped the flowers carelessly on the white-tiled counter. She did not miss the two wineglasses sitting in the sink along with a half-empty bottle of Chablis. Sara didn't know a great deal about wine, but she recognized the name on the label. I'll bet it was a very good year, she thought acidly.

Dingbat greeted her with his usual enthusiasm when she opened the door to her bedroom. Sara had grown quite fond of the big sheepdog, and she put aside her moodiness long enough to scratch his head before shooing him firmly out of the room so she could change.

Lydia Follett, she mused. I wonder what Mr. Follett does. I wonder if he knows his "insatiable" wife is spending "tantalizing" afternoons with a younger man?

Sara kicked off her high-heeled bone sandals and stripped off her dress. What did it matter anyway? She wasn't Matt Michael's keeper. She barely knew him. They were just two grown people who happened to be sharing the same apartment. What he did was his business.

Crossing to her closet, she pulled out a navy cotton T-shirt dress and tugged it on over her head. She was about to thrust her feet into a pair of rather battered espadrilles when there was a knock at the door.

"What?" she snapped.

The door opened and Matt stuck his head in. "Hi."

"I said 'what,' not 'come in.'"

"Sorry. But, since the damage is already done—" He opened the door completely and took a few steps into her bedroom. "I'm sorry about Lydia. I'd intended to have her out of here before you came home."

Sara put on the rope-trimmed canvas shoes and shut the closet. "There's nothing in our living arrangements that prohibits either of us from having guests over."

He gave her a sharp look. "We had a few things to catch up on."

"I think Mrs. Follett's phrase was 'you got carried away.'" Even to her own ears it sounded extremely bitchy. She saw Matt's eyes narrow suddenly. Swallowing, she looked away from him. "Forget I said that," she mumbled. "Your friend—she is very . . . stylish."

"Lydia is a lot of things. Including stylish."

Sara turned away. "Have you known her for a long time?" she asked in a tight voice. While she knew she should drop the subject, something inside her goaded her to ask the question.

"About ten years. She helped me get my start."

"She knew a good thing when she saw it, hmmm?" She folded the dress unthinkingly and placed it on the bed.

Moving swiftly and silently, Matt came up behind her before she realized what he was doing. He caught her by the shoulders and turned her around.

"What's eating you?" he demanded.

"Nothing." She stood very still, refusing to look up at him. Fixing her eyes stubbornly on his chest, she tried to shut her mind to the vividly remembered image of Lydia Follett's perfectly manicured hand touching Matt.

"Don't give me 'nothing.' You've been acting strangely since you walked in."

"Maybe that's because I didn't like what I walked in on!"

She sucked in her breath. She hadn't meant to say that. Not in a million years!

"Maybe you didn't—" Matt put one hand under her chin and forced her to meet his gaze. He studied her stormy expression for a long moment. She saw something very disturbing flicker in the mesmerizing cobalt depths of his eyes. "Could you be jealous?" he asked in a soft, wondering voice.

"Jealous? Don't be ridiculous!" It came out high-pitched and breathy. She jerked her face away.

"Ridiculous?" he challenged, catching her chin again.

"*Yes!* Of all the insufferably arrogant ideas—"

"You didn't mind seeing Lydia kiss me good-bye?"

"Why should I mind?" The faint lime scent of his after shave was in her nostrils along with the muskier, more basic smell of his skin. "What possible reason—"

"Well, for one thing, I'd be jealous if I came back to the apartment and found a man doing this to you."

"This" was a kiss of dizzying, devastating thoroughness. Matt began by brushing his mouth over hers in a teasing, tantalizing movement. After a moment Sara felt the quick, sweet stroke of his tongue. Her breath seemed to catch at the top of her throat. Her body began to respond even as her mind sent out frantic calls for resistance.

"Sweet Sara," Matt murmured huskily. Her lips parted. Whether it was in protest or invitation did not matter. He took skilled, seductive advantage of it and deepened the kiss, sipping and sampling the taste of her. The fingers that had been holding her chin slid up the smooth line of her jaw and moved to tangle in the silken curls of her hair. He cradled the back of her head in his palm, controlling the movements of her head. His other hand slipped from her shoulder down to her waist, holding her firm against him, making her vividly conscious of his arousal. She could feel the press and thrust of his hardness through the thin cotton of her dress.

Her own hands came up. She meant to push him away. Instead her palms settled flat against the warm, naked flesh of his hair-rough chest. Her fingertips accidentally touched the sensitive circles of his nipples. He shuddered a little, his tongue probing more demandingly into the moistly honeyed recesses of her mouth. She closed her eyes . . .

She felt the press of something against the back of her knees. A moment later Matt had tumbled her down onto the bed, their mouths fused in a kiss that was no longer one-sided.

Sara was trembling, half-eager, half-afraid. Anticipation warred with apprehension in her slender body.

Matt nipped gently at her lower lip, then placed a quick series of kisses on her chin and cheeks. Her eyes fluttered open in surprise when she felt the fleeting lick of his tongue on the bridge of her nose.

"Matt?" Her brain was whirling.

"Freckles," he said, his eyes gazing down into hers with the liquid glow of molten sapphires. "I noticed them that first morning when I came in to check on you. They're like a dusting of nutmeg on vanilla custard . . . very tempting."

He was the one who was tempting. Still a stranger, yet so familiar—

She gasped as she felt one of his hands stroke her side then move to caress the slim line of her thigh.

"I want to make love with you, Sara," he told her steadily. "You can feel that, can't you?" His fingers were playing at the edge of the hem of her dress, sending fiery prickles of excitement dancing up along the sensitive skin of her inner thighs.

Yes, she could feel his want . . . and the burgeoning of her own long-denied desires. A melting heat was washing through her bloodstream, bringing with it an aching need for completion. Yet, at the same time, she felt a

sense of wholeness she hadn't experienced since she'd
been shattered by the truth about Gary.

Gary!

She froze. What was she doing? She stared up into
Matt's lean-featured face in appalled disbelief.

"Sara?"

"I don't know you!" she got out.

"This is one very good way of getting acquainted."

She'd given herself—her virginity—to Gary Beaumont in an act of love and trust. In the end she had seen
that love destroyed and the trust betrayed. She neither
loved nor trusted Mathieson Michaels. Yet she had been
about to open herself to him in the most intimate, un-
guarded fashion. *What was she doing?*

"No." She shook her head from side to side. "I can't.
I don't want this, Matt."

She knew with shameful clarity that her last words
were a lie. She saw in the depths of his crystalline eyes
that he knew it too. She saw something else as well—
a dangerous stirring of an emotion that went far beyond
sexual frustration. For a moment Sara was genuinely
frightened. She was also aware of his superior strength
and size.

He expelled a harsh breath, making an angry sound
very like the one he had made when she flinched from
his touch that first night on the couch. His dark brows
came together in a brooding line as he released her and
sat up.

"Don't look at me like that," he said curtly. "If you
don't want it, sweetheart, neither do I. I've been guilty
of a lot of things in my life, but rape isn't one of them."
His eyes were hard as gemstones as they raked over her.
"I didn't figure you for a tease, Sara."

She sat up, too, tugging her dress down to cover an
immodestly revealed expanse of thigh. "I am not a tease,"
she denied shakenly. *"You* kissed *me!"*

"And you kissed me back."

"You started it."

"Just count yourself damn lucky I didn't finish it." He got to his feet and buttoned his shirt.

"What does that—"

"I'm going out," he said, cutting her off, as he headed for the bedroom door. "Don't hold dinner and don't wait up," he tossed over his shoulder, and he exited.

"Don't worry, I won't!"

A few moments later she heard the door to the apartment slam shut. The sound hit her like a slap in the face.

Damn him! Where did he get off acting as though what had happened was her doing? He was the one at fault!

Lifting an unsteady hand, Sara pressed her fingertips to her lips. She wanted to wipe off the tingle of Matt's ardent kiss, to blot out the lingering feel of his hard, compelling mouth on hers.

Had he kissed Lydia Follett like that? Had that been part of what she had found so "tantalizing."

Matt and an older woman. An older married woman who could obviously afford to indulge herself anyway she wanted to.

When Sara realized the shape her suspicions were taking, she recoiled.

"Strictly business," the blonde had said with a smile which, in retrospect, struck Sara as very proprietary. And just moments after that smile Lydia had told Matt she'd given his name to someone who wanted to pay him "lots of money."

"No!" Sara said aloud, shaking her head. Matt couldn't—wouldn't—be capable of that kind of cold-blooded commerce. She was certain of it. True, she'd known him for less than two weeks, but even on such a short acquaintance she couldn't believe—

You're not the best judge of character when it comes to men, are you? Chrissie's heedless, hurtful words echoed tauntingly through her head.

Sara clenched her hands into fists, her fingernails biting into her palms. She swung her legs off the bed. No, she wasn't the "best" judge. But she was better at it now than she had been back in Syracuse, thanks to Gary. She'd been certain that he wasn't capable of dishonesty and betrayal, so certain that she'd come very close to compromising her own integrity.

And she'd been so certain because she'd loved him . . . or thought she'd loved him.

Could she possibly—? No! There was no way in the world she could be anywhere near in love with Mathieson Michaels. All right, she was attracted to him. And intrigued by him. But in love? The idea was ridiculous; it was as ridiculous as his egotistical suggestion that she was jealous of Lydia.

"Oh, what do I care?" she exclaimed forcefully. She started as Dingbat punctuated her outburst with a loud bark from the doorway. Despite herself, Sara gave a reluctant laugh when she realized the animal had brought his feeding dish with him. "You don't care, do you, Ding?" she asked, sliding off the bed. "You just want your dinner, don't you?"

The dog barked in apparent agreement and nosed the dish pointedly.

"Okay, okay." She smoothed her T-shirt dress with her palms. She then straightened the mussed-up coverlet on her bed, determinedly erasing all traces of the brief moment of passion she had experienced with Matt.

Where had he and Lydia—?

She sucked in her breath angrily. Whatever Matt had done with Lydia—and whether he had done it for love, money, or something else—she didn't want to think about the details. At least they'd stayed out of her room!

She recalled Matt's provocative, teasing remark about using the living room once a week for an orgy—and about her being welcome to join in. At the time she had thought it was just an outrageous way of baiting her.

Now, to her bitter dismay, she was beginning to wonder.

With swishing tail and snuffling reminders that it was his dinnertime, the sheepdog followed Sara out of the bedroom. Matt was well and truly gone. The apartment felt strangely empty because of it. Odd, how his vibrant presence seemed to fill the place when he was there.

"Where do you think he went, Ding?" she asked the dog as she crossed the living room. She checked herself in midstep as she saw what was lying on one of the white lacquered end tables by the gray sectional sofa in the center of the room. It was Matt's crowded key ring. The same key ring he had dangled before her so triumphantly that first night.

Wherever Matt had gone, he was going to have trouble getting back into the apartment. So much for angry exits, she thought with a spiteful trace of satisfaction, and headed for the kitchen.

After dishing out a heaping serving of dog food for Dingbat, Sara turned her attention to her own dinner. A hunt through the refrigerator turned up nothing that piqued her curiously diminished appetite. A search through the cabinets was even less productive.

She *had* kissed him back. She'd kissed him back, and God knew how much more she might have done if she hadn't come to her senses. If putting a stop to something that never should have gotten started in the first place made her a tease, so be it.

Did Matt really think such an awful thing of her?

When Sara moved back into the living room, she was carrying a glass and a plate laden with a handful of crackers, a hunk of cheddar cheese, and several slices of pepperoni. She had the half-empty bottle of Chablis tucked underneath her right arm.

Matt would cool down and come back. When he did, she'd behave like the mature twenty-eight-year-old woman she was and let him in the apartment. He'd apologize . . . and so would she.

The crackers turned out to be stale and the cheese tasted like orange rubber. After one tentative nibble Sara decided she hated pepperoni.

The wine did not make her silly or sleepy; but it did make her sad.

Chapter 4

"UMPH." SARA SHIFTED restlessly. How was she supposed to sleep with Matt shaking her by the shoulders and saying her name in that soft, velvety voice?

"Sara."

He was saying it again! Didn't he know it was the middle of the night? Didn't he know he was supposed to be locked out of the apartment? Didn't he know that the only way he was going to get back inside was if she let him in?

She hadn't let him in. She would have remembered doing that. Then what was he doing—?

Sara opened her eyes, a peculiar sense of déjà vu washing over her. She was lying on the sofa and Matt was bending over her.

"What are you doing here?" she asked. There was a soft flush on her cheeks and her glossy cap of auburn hair was a tumble of uncontrolled curls.

"I live here."

"I know that." She blinked and glanced toward the foyer in speculation. "You broke in, didn't you?"

Matt smiled, an amused sparkle appearing in his eyes. "Didn't we have this conversation once before? About two weeks ago?"

"You had a set of keys with you then. You left your keys here tonight." Stifling a yawn, she sat up. Looking down, she realized her dress had ridden up. She bit her lip in irritation and tugged at the offending garment until she was properly covered again.

With infuriating courtesy Matt waited for Sara to finish rearranging her clothes before speaking. His steady gaze did not stray from her face.

"I cannot tell a lie," he said. "I used a credit card to get in."

"A credit card?"

"The lock on the door is very easy to slip with a piece of plastic. That's why there's a deadbolt. Which didn't happen to be thrown, Sara."

"You know how to pick locks?" she probed, ignoring the censure in his tone.

"It's not a major intellectual accomplishment."

"I don't know how to do it. And you're the first person I've ever met who admitted he did." Lock picking was an odd type of skill for someone to have at his or her fingertips.

"If you want, I'll teach you. I'll also give you a free demonstration on how to put on the security bolt."

"I already know how to do that," she informed him tartly.

"Then why didn't you?"

"Don't lecture me!"

"I'm not lecturing you. I'm worrying about you."

Sara sniffed. "Don't bother. I can take care of myself."

"With your faithful squash racquet, I suppose?" he countered sarcastically. "Sara, did you ever stop to think about what would have happened that first night if I'd turned out to be a genuine intruder?" He was grimly serious.

"I—" Unfortunately, he had a point. She tacitly admitted this by trying to redirect the conversation. "I was going to put on the bolt when I went to bed."

For a moment she thought he would pursue his line of questioning. Then, surprisingly, his expression lightened. "And just when were you going to do that? It's nearly midnight now." He paused before inquiring silkily, "You weren't waiting up for me by any chance?"

"No!" she stiffened, her indignation at this suggestion overcoming her very natural curiosity about where he had been for the past five hours. "I was...eating my dinner." She pointed to the end table where she had deposited the plate, glass, and now-empty wine bottle.

Matt studied the remains of her evening meal in silence for at least ten seconds. Sara knew he was deliberately trying to aggravate her. She also knew he was succeeding.

"Are you sure you weren't drinking *my* Chablis?" he asked pleasantly.

"I...may have had a glass," she conceded primly.

"Or two," he amended in the same exasperatingly amiable voice he had used before.

"What were you doing?" she challenged. "Saving it for Mrs. Follett's next visit?"

"Sara." Matt sighed, leaning back against the sofa and running a hand through his dark, disordered hair. "Just forget about Lydia, please? I don't want to fight with you. I apologize for what happened earlier. I guess I got—"

"Don't say 'carried away,'" she warned him. She'd taken an irrational dislike to the phrase.

He grinned briefly but with a warmth that sent a very pleasurable shiver running through her. Reaching out, he stroked a casual finger down her cheek.

"Things got out of hand," he continued. "I lost my temper and I'm sorry. I wouldn't hurt you for the world, Sara. Believe me."

She found herself fighting a desire to touch him in return, to brush back the comma of black hair that curved down over his forehead. "I believe you," she said quietly. "And I'm sorry, too, about what happened."

He nodded. "Good." After a moment he stood up in a lithe movement and regarded her quizzically. "Now, do you want something to eat or do you want to go to bed?"

Sara laughed and got up off the sofa. "I want to go to bed," she announced with a cheeky smile. "And you can throw the deadbolt on the door since you're such an expert."

"You're in a good mood," Matt observed late the next morning when Sara strolled into the kitchen, humming. He was sitting at the butcher block table in the center of the room, a mug of coffee and a half-eaten croissant at his elbow and *The New York Times* spread out in front of him. Pen in hand, he was working on the crossword puzzle.

"Why shouldn't I be?" she inquired, stooping to give Ding a friendly pat on the head. "It's a gorgeous summer Saturday." As she rose gracefully she caught sight of something that made her eyes widen in delighted surprise. Matt's black lacquer vase was sitting on the counter by the sink. It was filled with her red and white carnations.

"And what do you have to do this gorgeous summer Saturday?"

Sara crossed to the refrigerator. In addition to being in a cheerful mood, she was very hungry. She opened the icebox and took out a container of grapefruit juice. Retrieving a glass from the dishwasher, she poured herself a serving. She then gulped down half of it, enjoying the cold, tart liquid.

"I don't have to do anything," she declared blithely. "Except eat. I am absolutely starving this morning." She looked into the refrigerator again. Chunky peanut butter on a croissant seemed very appealing to her at the moment.

"I was afraid you might be absolutely hung over after last night," Matt commented dryly.

Sara decided to settle for a croissant with butter and raspberry jam. She shut the refrigerator. "I have a very hard head," she replied easily, refusing to rise to the bait. She brought her juice, two croissants, and the jar of jam over to the table. Sitting down, she watched silently as he filled in a row of blank spaces on the puzzle. His printing had a bold, angular precision.

Sara reached for the butter. "You know," she remarked sweetly, "I've always thought that there was something arrogant about people who do crossword puzzles—especially the *Times* crossword puzzle—in ink."

Matt glanced at her, one brow cocked. Amusement tugged at the corners of his lips, deepening the faint grooves that ran from his nose to his mouth. "People who work crossword puzzles in ink generally know what they're doing," he responded.

"Is that where you found out about phrenology?" She spread a liberal portion of butter on the corner of one roll, then added a generous smear of jam.

"Phrenology?" He wrote in another answer.

"You remember, the arcane art of reading the bumps on a person's skull. You told me the night we met that having felt the lumps on my head, you knew my most intimate secrets." She took a bite of croissant and chewed it with a teasingly thoughtful expression. "Phrenology sounds like a word you'd find in a crossword puzzle."

"I found out about phrenology from a very old gypsy

woman here in New York. She used to work way down on the Lower East Side. And it was a scam . . . as I seem to recall your suggesting."

"Then you *don't* know my most intimate secrets?" She ate more of the roll.

To her surprise, Matt suddenly reached across the table and wiped at the corner of her mouth with one finger.

"Jam," he explained, licking the finger clean with a quick movement of his tongue. Feeling strangely warm-cheeked, Sara rubbed self-consciously at her mouth with the back of one hand. She then took a deep drink of juice. "And no, I don't know your most intimate se-crets—yet. I'm working on it. Besides, you don't know mine, either."

"Ummm . . ." Sara made a noise she hoped sounded suitably noncommittal. She was beginning to think that she'd better tone down her summer Saturday ebullience before she got into trouble.

"One not so intimate secret, in case you're interested," he said, folding up the paper. "I like your outfit. You look like a pastel parfait."

"Thank you," Sara replied, flattered by the unexpected compliment. She was wearing a flouncy peach-and-white Liberty print skirt and a sleeveless white knit top. A wide woven belt emphasized the slimness of her waist, and the lace-up ties on her sandals enhanced the shapely length of her legs. The overall look was a definite de-parture from her normal "sensible Sara" style.

"You're welcome."

"Do you have anything to do today?" She polished off the croissant with a satisfied sigh.

"I thought I might spend it with you."

"Me?" She was genuinely surprised. "You want us—"

"We can take Dingbat along as a chaperone," he of-fered.

"But what would we do?"

"With Ding along, not much." He grinned briefly. "I really would like to spend the day with you Sara," he added after a moment, his blue eyes steady.

Sara hesitated, toying with her juice glass. It wasn't that she found the prospect of being with Matt unpleasant. Quite the contrary, the idea was very appealing.

Maybe a bit too appealing, a small voice warned her.

"Sensible Sara" probably would have listened to that voice. But it was a gorgeous summer day and Sara wasn't feeling particularly sensible at the moment.

"I'd like to spend the day with you, too, Matt," she said. "But without Dingbat."

The weather was gloriously clear and sunny but not too hot. Overhead, the sky was as blue as Matt's eyes, dotted here and there with small puffs of marshmallow-white clouds.

They began by strolling west, talking of inconsequential things. Sara had read an article about a special retrospective showing at the Metropolitan Museum of Art, and she'd suggested they might start their day together there.

The museum stood, in impressive stone splendor, on Fifth Avenue at Eighty-second Street. The huge expanse of stairs leading up to the entrance was bustling with people. Gaily colored banners announcing some of the current exhibits hung on the front of the building, fluttering in the breeze.

It took Sara just a few seconds to decide that for today at least she preferred the scene outside the museum to the displays within. Matt cheerfully agreed with her assertion that great art was best appreciated on rainy Sunday afternoons.

Two mimes were performing off to the side at the foot of the steps. Clad all in black except for garishly striped vests, they delighted a crowd of children and adults with their silent antics. They drew repeated bursts of laughter and applause as they balanced on invisible tightropes and leaned nonchalantly against objects that weren't there. Sara, like the rest of the audience, was quick to come up with a few coins when the mimes passed the hat at the end of their impromptu show.

Afterwards Matt grabbed her hand and they dashed to catch the Fifth Avenue bus. Once on board, Sara scrabbled in her roomy white straw shoulder bag for the correct fare. While she was still searching, Matt calmly produced two tokens from his jeans pocket and dropped them into the fare box. He then took Sara's hand again and led her back to an unoccupied pair of seats near the middle of the bus.

Sara's first impulse once they sat down was to pull her hand free of Matt's. Then she realized that the female riders seated across from them were devouring Matt with their avid stares. The women were in their mid-twenties, chicly dressed, and they were gazing at Matt like two deprived chocolate lovers who have just spotted a huge serving of chocolate-chocolate-chip ice cream slathered in hot fudge sauce.

Prompted by a spurt of emotion she didn't want to examine too closely right then, Sara very casually let her slender fingers intertwine with Matt's leanly powerful ones. She couldn't really blame the women for staring. Matt had a magnetic quality that went far beyond his lithe, virile physique or his rakishly attractive looks.

He didn't flaunt his masculinity; it was simply an ingrained, incontrovertible part of him. There were other more classically handsome or better-dressed men on the bus, but they somehow faded in comparison with Matt.

They got off at a stop near the famed Plaza Hotel. Sara looked longingly at the old-fashioned hansom cabs standing along the curb at the corner of Central Park South and Fifth Avenue. The horses seemed undisturbed by the city noise and traffic, slowly switching their tails back and forth to ward off flies while they dug deep into their feedbags. Scores of pigeons strutted about on the pavement, pecking up the crumbs of grain dropped by the animals.

"Have you ever ridden in a hansom cab?" she asked Matt with a trace of wistfulness. She smiled delightedly as one of the drivers—a young man dressed in bluejeans and a lavishly embroidered and patched dinner jacket—tipped his tophat to her with a theatrical flourish.

"Never. But I think it's the sort of thing we should save for a beautiful moonlit night."

"Oh, yes." His casual use of the word *we* sent a sweet but disturbing shiver of anticipation running through her.

"I've got a better idea at the moment." There was a roguish gleam in his eye as he spoke.

"You do?"

"Umm-hmm. F.A.O. Schwarz." He pointed toward the opposite corner. "Let's go buy Ding a toy to make up for leaving him at home today. Come on."

Laughing her agreement, Sara joined him in running across Fifth Avenue, just narrowly escaping a brush with a cab.

"Careful," Matt warned. "Don't you know better than to play chicken with a New York taxi driver?"

"Sorry."

Buying a present for Dingbat might have been Matt's stated reason for visiting the well-known toy store, but Sara quickly made up her mind it was all a ruse.

"You're worse than an eight-year-old boy!" she hissed at him as he began tickling her with a monkey hand puppet.

"That's because I've had time to learn a lot of things no eight-year-old boy could possibly know." He lifted his brows significantly. "I'm all grown up, in case you haven't noticed."

"Matt!" The monkey was now nuzzling amorously at

her ear. She brushed at the plush-covered puppet. "Stop it."

"What's wrong? Don't you like monkeying around?"

Sara groaned at the pun. She retaliated by picking up an alligator puppet and nipping Matt's nose with it.

"Excuse me," a polite voice interrupted. "May I help you with something?"

Feeling like a naughty little girl, Sara turned to confront a neatly dressed middle-aged salesclerk. The woman was regarding her with a tolerant twinkle. She looked as though she were accustomed to adults who reverted to childhood within moments of stepping into Schwarz's toyland.

"Uh...er—" Sara stammered.

"We're just browsing," Matt cut in with a flashing smile. The woman's twinkle brightened considerably. "My friend was looking for something to do with her hands." He favored Sara with a glance of pseudo-compassionate understanding. "Thank you for asking."

"Well, if there's anything I can do, just ask," the clerk said, nodding.

After a few more minutes of shopping around they purchased a fire-engine-red ball for Dingbat. Once it was properly wrapped, Sara put the toy into her oversize purse.

"Your shoulder bag looks like it's pregnant," Matt commented as he held the door for her.

"Do you want to carry the ball?" she countered, tossing her mahogany curls as she stepped out into the sunshine.

"No, I'll leave it in your very capable hands."

From F.A.O. Schwarz they took a leisurely walk down Fifth Avenue, glancing at the displays in the various shops along their route. Matt had taken a pair of wire-rimmed sunglasses from his back jeans pocket and put them on. They gave him an air of guarded inaccessability. Squinting a bit, Sara found herself wishing that she, too, had something with which to shade her eyes against the glare of the summer sun.

"You need one of those," Matt announced suddenly, nodding toward a mannequin in the window of Saks Fifth Avenue.

"One of what?" Sara asked. The mannequin—an impossibly thin representation of the female form—was clothed in a singularly abbreviated swimsuit. "There isn't enough fabric in that to qualify as one of anything."

"Not the suit—although I wouldn't mind seeing you in it. I'm talking about the hat."

The hat was a very pretty, wide-brimmed confection made of white straw. The crown was ringed with small silk flowers and a coral satin ribbon that trailed flirtatiously down the back.

"Oh, Matt, that's really not my type of thing," she said doubtfully.

"Maybe not, but it's mine. Humor me, Sara. It will look great with what you're wearing . . . and keep the sun out of your eyes."

Matt's coaxing expression was difficult to resist. The feel of his hand cupping her elbow and steering her into the store decided the matter. When they emerged some twenty minutes later, Sara was the owner of a new hat, paid for, over her protests, by her apartmentmate.

"All right, all right! I'll accept the hat. But I have to buy lunch."

"Are you hungry again?" he jibed, flipping one of the hat's fluttering ribbons back over her shoulder.

"I never stopped being hungry. Besides, it's past one already."

"Okay. If you like Chinese food, I know a place downtown that serves great dim sum on the weekends."

"Dim what?"

"Dumplings to you, Sara."

"Dumplings to you, too."

* * *

The restaurant was situated in a very unprepossessing alley in Chinatown. Matt navigated the route from the subway with the air of a man who knew precisely where he was going. Sara had only been down to this section of Manhattan once before, and she had been more than a little confused by the twisting streets and exotic atmosphere.

A dim sum meal, she swiftly learned, was an informal and rather adventurous affair. Every few minutes, it seemed, the restaurant's kitchen door swung open and an aproned waiter came whizzing out pushing a rolling cart laden with a new supply of savory tidbits. The waiter then barreled around the dining room, doling out his dumplings to anyone who indicated an interest.

Half the time Sara wasn't certain what she was eating, but she didn't seek enlightenment. Enjoying some unknown, unusual-tasting delicacy was one thing. Finding out she had just bitten into something called a sea slug was entirely another.

Over the course of their meal Sara and Matt munched their way through delicately fried egg rolls filled with shrimp, bean sprouts, and minced mushrooms; steamed vegetable dumplings done up in fluted white noodle wrappers; and boiled pork pastries. Some of the items offered looked like puffy white tennis balls; others were golden brown cylinders. A number of the dim sum came with special dipping sauces that ranged from a mellow sweet-plum concoction to a blazingly spicy liquid that tasted like essence of chili peppers.

Sara shook her head to something that bore a very definite resemblance to petrified duck feet. She also decided—despite Matt's grinning assurances—that she could do without a dumpling called "dog won't leave."

By the time they finished their table was littered with more than a dozen small dishes. This, Sara discovered, was how their bill was figured out. After counting the dishes and making a few impossible-to-read scribbles on a piece of paper, their waiter presented them with the bill.

They spent another hour walking around, exploring and talking. While Matt continued to be reticent about his background, Sara did learn a few things about him. His father was a wealthy businessman who died of a heart attack when Matt was eleven. Matt had been expelled from at least one exclusive boys' school and had never finished college. And he was a man who preferred to go his own way in the world . . . traveling far, fast, and free.

Finally, late in the afternoon, they descended the steps to a subway station to head back uptown. After depositing their fares and pushing through the metal turnstiles, they moved out onto the platform to wait for their train.

"Do you think Ding will like his present?" Sara asked.

"He'll love it once he gets over the disappointment of discovering he can't eat it." Matt smiled.

Sara smiled back. "I like my present," she told him, patting the brim of her hat.

"And you look positively edible in it," he returned. "In fact—"

"Well, well, Matty, it *is* you," a deep, somewhat hoarse voice interrupted from behind them. Sara was standing so close to Matt that she could feel his body tense at the first sound of the grating voice. They both turned.

The man who had spoken appeared to be in his early forties. He was a bit taller than Matt and much heavier. He was built along very beefy, muscular lines and was wearing tan knit slacks, a white open-collared shirt, and a plaid sports jacket that seemed strained to the bursting point by his broad shoulders and powerful forearms. His short, thinning hair was light brown, his eyes were a flat slate gray, and his nose appeared to have been "rear-ranged" on several occasions without benefit of a plastic surgeon.

He looks like he could punch down a door, Sara thought with a tremor of alarm as she glanced at the man's ham-like hands. Or maybe he could batter it down with his head.

She shot a questioning look at Matt. To her astonishment, he started to chuckle.

"Tank!" he exclaimed, extending his hand. The other man clasped it briefly in what Sara suspected was a potentially bone-crushing grip.

"You're getting damn careless, man," the brawny man said in a reproving rumble. "I picked you up five or ten minutes ago. Hell, you were barely looking where you were going! Then you let me come up in back of you the way you did." He shook his head, his gray eyes turning significantly toward Sara. "Matty, Matty, you can't let yourself get so distracted."

Matt's chuckle turned into a genuine laugh. While he seemed truly pleased to see this "Tank," Sara thought she detected a hint of constraint in his manner.

"You're always looking out for me, Tank," Matt returned. He slipped an arm casually around Sara's waist. "Well, at least let me introduce you to my distraction. Sara, this is De—"

"Tank Petrie," the other man bulldozed in. "No need to get fancy. I'm a low-profile kind of guy these days."

Sara saw blue eyes meet gray. The contact lasted only a moment, but she knew some kind of message had been exchanged.

"Right," Matt agreed easily, his expression just a shade too bland. "You always did have a knack for blending into the woodwork. Who notices a walking mountain? In any case, Sara, this is Tank Petrie, an old friend. Tank, this is Sara Edwards, a new friend."

In a bizarre way the situation reminded Sara of her meeting with Lydia Follett the day before. Smiling briefly, she murmured a polite hello. Tank responded with a gruff greeting, his eyes running over her. Sara wasn't offended by his assessment—it was too impersonal for that. But the thoroughness of the inspection did make her uncomfortable.

"So, Tank," Matt said, still keeping Sara close to him, "when did they turn you loose?"

"About two months ago. And man, let me tell you, it's good to be back out on the streets."

"You couldn't take it on the inside, hmmm?"

Tank showed his teeth in a crooked grin. "I developed some very heavy attitude and adjustment problems," he announced in a flippant tone. "What about you? Still telling lies for a living?"

Sara felt her stomach knot.

"You have such a way with words, Tank," Matt commented. "But, yeah, I'm still in the same line." Matt's blue eyes met Tank's gray again; message sent, received, and understood.

Tank looked away first, surveying the subway platform as he rocked back on his feet. Despite his bulk, he gave off a curious impression of quickness.

"You been back in town long, Matty?" he inquired, thrusting his hands into his pants pockets.

"A few weeks."

"Well, some of your old cruising buddies might like to see you again. Did you ever consider that?"

"I'll be around, Tank. I'm busy with a few things right now."

Tank took a moment to think this over. "Sure, I can see that," he replied dryly. "You want me to keep my trap shut about running into you?"

"I'd appreciate it."

"Okay." Tank cocked his head. "Sounds like your train," he commented offhandedly. "One thing you should know. Santini's been asking questions about you. I think somebody spilled at least some of the beans to him."

"Great. Now he'll be all over me." Matt sounded disgusted by the prospect.

"Hey, Matty, he was bound to stumble into it. The guy doesn't exactly believe in Santa Claus, you know."

"True. Well, thanks for the warning." He paused as the rushing clatter of metal on metal announced the imminent approach of their subway train. "You watch out for yourself, Tank."

"I always do, man." He showed his teeth again. "Nice to make your acquaintance, Sara."

"I—I'm pleased to have met you, too, Mr.—er—Tank," she responded.

The train came screeching to a halt at the platform at that point. Tank lifted his hand in a casual farewell and ambled away. After a moment Matt and Sara boarded one of the graffiti-covered cars. About a minute later there was a grinding noise and the train lurched out of the station.

Sara's mind was whirling with the implications of the conversation she had just heard. There were dozens of questions troubling her, but something made her hold back from asking them.

What had Chrissie overheard Lowell saying? Something about Matt's having disgraced the family name with his low-life connections? Was Tank Petrie one of those connections?

He certainly looked the part. Sara could very easily imagine him threatening to break someone's kneecaps. Tank Petrie was definitely *not* the sort of man a person would want to be alone with in a dark alley!

And the way he talked! Lord, it sounded like dialogue from a crime melodrama.

Beyond that—who was Santini? Why was he asking about Matt? What beans had there been for somebody to spill?

"Sara?"

She started, going pale as Matt tilted back the brim of her hat.

"Sara, are you all right?"

"Matt—" She swallowed hard. Her hazel eyes were wide and searching. "Matt, are you in some kind of trouble?"

"Trouble?" His blue eyes narrowed. They held a mixture of surprise, wariness, and something else she couldn't decipher.

"Are you?"

"Whatever—oh, Tank's crack about Santini!" He shook his dark head. "That's just the way he talks. It's okay."

He was evading her, and it was not okay.

"But if this Santini is asking about you—"

He put his fingers to her lips, stopping the question.

"Sara, it's a simple matter of some unfinished personal business. Nothing serious. I arranged to put up the money for something that Santini wasn't supposed to find out about."

Arranged to put up . . . bail money! Lowell had been arguing with Matt about bail money, hadn't he?

Sara averted her head a little, her mouth tingling from his touch. She forced herself to hide her distress.

"Tank said . . . he thinks Santini's found out," she said evenly.

She felt Matt shrug. "I guess it was inevitable. He's a hard man to keep secrets from. But don't worry about it. I can handle him." He reached over and caught her chin, turning her back to face him. He was smiling. "If worse comes to worst, and he should track me down to the apartment, you can go after him with your squash racquet. Okay?"

Sara managed a small, surprisingly convincing laugh. Inside, she felt sick and more than a little scared. She was frightened not for herself, but for Matt. "Okay," she said.

Two days later a man named Santini knocked on the door of the apartment.

Chapter 5

IT HAD NOT been the best of Mondays to begin with. After the glorious weather of the weekend, the skies had opened up with a summer downpour of torrential force. The storm underscored Sara's unsettled mood.

Her workday had consisted of a niggling series of crises punctuated by a traumatic two-hour session with a client who had received notice he was being audited by the Internal Revenue Service. The man was reacting with panicky indignation.

The accountant who had prepared the man's return was no longer with the firm. Although Sara did not specialize in tax work, she was tapped to deal with the situation. She suspected her superiors wanted to see how she would handle a difficult case.

After reviewing the pertinent forms and financial records, she felt confident the client had nothing to worry about. The man was in a high tax bracket, and she knew the IRS computer randomly kicked out a certain percentage of high-income returns each year for routine audits. It seemed likely that that was what had happened in this case.

Unfortunately, the man wasn't soothed by this explanation—or by Sara's very professional reassurances. She had gone over his forms line by line, frequently citing applicable portions of the tax code, but it had not helped very much. She'd finally sent the man away with the suggestion that he have at least one stiff drink before they met to go to his audit at the specified time, date, and location. She was not looking forward to *that* session. Even though the man's taxes were in impeccable order, she was afraid he would confess to some wrongdoing, just because he was so intimidated by the idea of undergoing IRS scrutiny.

Elayne begged off from their usual Monday night squash game. It seemed one of her agency's biggest clients was developing cold feet about buying commercial time on a controversial television miniseries, and she was caught in the middle of the mess. Sara suggested that her friend have at least one stiff drink, too. Elayne said that she already had.

Despite the protection of her umbrella and beige poplin raincoat, Sara was pretty well drenched by the time she got home. Given her rotten state of mind, it somehow seemed appropriate. As she stood just inside the apartment door, dripping all over the polished parquet floor, she decided *she* was the one who should have at least one stiff drink.

"Matt?" she called, feeling a peculiar prickle of alarm. Even as she spoke his name she knew he wasn't there.

They'd spent a perfectly amiable evening together Saturday after their sightseeing expedition, and had gone to a double feature of *The Maltese Falcon* and *Casablanca* at a West Side revival house on Sunday. Afterward Sara had the uneasy sense that there was something rather ominous about their choice of films.

Matt had been up and out with Dingbat Monday morning when she awoke. There was nothing unusual in that. What *was* unusual was that he hadn't returned by the time she left for work. Telling herself that the pace of his daily run had probably been slowed by the bad weather, Sara had gone off, leaving a scrawled note of greeting on the refrigerator door.

She had tried calling the apartment twice during the day—something she had never done before—and gotten no answer.

"Matt?" she repeated, pulling off her raincoat. She grimaced as a dribble of water ran down her nose, and then she kicked off her sodden shoes.

Dingbat suddenly poked his nose out of the door of the spare room at the end of the foyer. After a *woof-woof* of hello, he padded down to Sara, presenting himself for his customary dose of petting and ear scratching.

"Are you the only one home, boy?" she asked. "Did Matt go out and leave you alone?" Dingbat licked her hands. "Did he leave a message for me?"

Leaving a trail of damp footprints and drips behind her, Sara went into the kitchen. The black lacquer vase containing her carnations was sitting on the butcher-block table. She flicked one of the red-fringed blossoms with a casual finger and looked around.

There was a message taped to the slick white surface of the refrigerator. She crossed the room and pulled the slip of paper free.

Gone out. Be back about nine, Matt had written in his strong, angular script. *We have to talk.*

The last sentence was underlined.

"Talk about what?" Sara wondered aloud, frowning. She shivered a little as Dingbat nuzzled at the back of her legs. Glancing down, she saw the sheepdog had produced his red ball from somewhere. The present had proven a great success . . . even if it couldn't be eaten.

The animal barked hopefully.

"I can't play with you just now, Ding. I've got to get out of these wet clothes."

Where had Matt gone? she asked herself as she gave the dog an absentminded pat and headed into her bedroom. And *why* did they suddenly "have" to talk?

After stripping off her wet clothes Sara went into the bathroom. Matt's red toothbrush was in its usual place. His navy terry cloth robe—a recent purchase he'd termed one of his concessions to her modesty—hung on the hook on the back of the door. The faint scent of his after shave lingered in the air.

Sara glanced at herself in the mirror over the sink. The rain had washed away most of her makeup, revealing her fresh, creamy complexion... and the freckles on her nose. Thankfully, the mascara that coated her long lashes was waterproof and she'd been spared the indignity of dark brown rivulets coursing down her cheeks.

She showered, then shampooed her hair, using a lemon-scented finishing rinse. After towelling dry she spent a frustrating fifteen minutes trying to tame her hair with a dryer and brush. Ultimately, she decided she could live with the wild disorder of natural curls for one night. She'd use hot rollers in the morning.

Returning to her bedroom, she pulled on a persimmon knit tank top and a pair of white shorts. Then she went back into the kitchen. She discovered that Dingbat had deposited his ball in his feeding dish and had positioned both items—and himself—directly next to the cabinet where his food was kept.

Sara took the hint and served him his dinner. Checking the refrigerator, she found half a canteloupe. She put it in a bowl, filled the center with a generous scoop of cottage cheese, then adjourned to the living room.

She'd just finished spooning up the last bite of the sweet juicy melon and was about to switch on a news program when there was a knock at the door.

Matt! That was Sara's first reaction. Uncurling herself

from the corner of the sofa, she went to answer the summons. Dingbat beat her by a second, snuffling suspiciously.

Sara peered through the peephole. The man on the other side of the door was a complete stranger. He was of medium height and medium build, dressed in a dark raincoat. His dark brown hair was liberally streaked with gray, and he had a tough, lived-in-looking face. She watched as he rapped on the door again, his square jaw set in pugnacious determination.

"Who—who is it?" she asked finally.

"Lieutenant Joseph Santini, NYPD," came the uncompromising reply.

"Police?" Sara managed to get out after a moment. Oh, God, *this* was Santini! A New York City policeman! She felt cold all over.

"That's right, ma'am. I'd like a few words with you, please."

Dingbat barked loudly.

Sara cleared her throat. "I—I want to see some identification, please," she said. "You can hold it up to the peephole."

The man complied, showing her a pictured identification card and a badge. His movements were unhurried and deliberate.

The picture matched and the name on the card read LT. JOSEPH A. SANTINI. The badge, as far as she could tell, was genuine.

"Satisfied, ma'am?"

"Just a moment, please." The sheepdog was frisking around. Sara ordered him to sit, which he did, his tail thumping on the floor. Taking a steadying breath, she pasted what she hoped was a calmly inquiring look on her face and opened the door. "Yes, Lieutenant?"

He had dark, cynical eyes, with a network of fine wrinkles at the corners. He looked her up and down, then glanced beyond her as though taking some kind of inventory. A moment later his gaze settled on Dingbat. He shook his head.

"Damn if that dog hasn't gotten bigger," he said. "What is Michaels feeding him? Shetland pony chow?"

"M—Michaels?" She had trouble saying the name.

The policeman's momentary jocularity vanished. "May I at least come in, Miss—?"

"Edwards," she supplied, stepping back. He entered the apartment, pulling the door shut behind him.

"Edwards," he repeated.

"Ah—yes." She tilted her chin slightly. "Am I in some sort of trouble, Lieutenant Santini?"

"Not at all. In fact, I wouldn't be bothering you if we didn't have an acquaintance in common—Matt Michaels. I understand you're living with him."

For a moment Sara considered denying anything of the sort, but she quickly realized the foolishness of such a move. Santini obviously didn't just understand that Matt lived in the apartment with her... he *knew*.

"Matt Michaels and I are sharing this apartment for the summer," she said coolly. "We go our separate ways."

The policeman made a neutral noise. "I want to talk with him."

"I'm afraid that's impossible."

"Oh?"

"He's not here."

Santini shrugged slightly. "That's okay. I'm off duty. I can wait."

"He—I don't know when he'll be back." Her heart was pounding. "He—Matt's gone out of town."

The dark eyes narrowed. "Did he tell you to say that?"

"No!" Sara latched on to the chance to tell the truth with a sense of relief. Her eyes flared green with indignation. "No, Lieutenant, he did not tell me to say *anything!*"

Santini seemed to mull this over. "He's gone out of

town and you don't know when he'll be back," he said
slowly.

"That's right. And I don't know where he went, either."

"Was this a sudden thing? His going out of town, I
mean."

"He was gone when I got up this morning," she told
him with perfect accuracy.

The policeman expelled a long breath. "Okay, Miss
Edwards," he said finally, reaching into his raincoat. Sara
flinched instinctively, wondering if he was going to pull
out a gun. She came close to collapsing when he withdrew a small white rectangle and handed it to her. "This
is my card. When your roommate shows up, I'd like you
to call me. I'd also like you to give him a message."

Sara's skimpy top and brief shorts did not come
equipped with pockets. She was forced to hang on to the
business card and hope Santini didn't notice how badly
her hands were shaking.

"I'd be glad to ... give Matt your message."

"Just tell him Santini knows about the money."

"All right," She nodded her head.

"Then tell him to remember I'm part-Sicilian."

"P-part ... Sicilian," Sara echoed faintly.

Oh, God, she had lied to a policeman! She had deliberately, repeatedly *lied* ... and if she had it to do over
again, she would do the same thing. She would do it
again because, despite his casual denials on Saturday,
Matt Michaels was very definitely in trouble and she
wanted to help him.

She had to help him.

Where was he? She asked herself that question over
and over again as the clock crept toward nine o'clock at
an agonizingly slow pace.

Why did he have to be so secretive? So damnably

elusive? She had absolutely no idea of how to reach him. She had no idea of whom he saw or what he did when he left the apartment.

Lydia Follett. Tank Petrie. Lieutenant Joseph A. Santini.

A wealthy married woman who did "tantalizing business" in the afternoon with a younger man.

A tough hulk of a man who was glad to be "back on the streets."

And a New York police lieutenant who warned he was part-Sicilian... and knew about "the money."

All three had something in common: Matt Michaels.

Sara closed her eyes for a moment. Chrissie had accused her of not being a very good judge of men. That was true where Gary had been concerned. But with Matt... with Matt, Sara's emotional alarm system had been sending out warnings from the very first. She had judged him all too well, and despite that judgment—

Her eyes flew open as she heard the sound of a key being inserted into a lock. Her pulse pounding thunderously, she sprang up out of the chair where she had been sitting in between agitated bouts of pacing, raced to the door, and flung it open.

Matt was standing there wearing jeans, a light blue work shirt, and an unbuttoned tan trench coat. His dark wavy hair was damp, and there seemed to be a raindrop or two clinging to his absurdly long lashes.

Sara's throat closed up. For a moment she was afraid she might start to cry with relief or pass out from the stress of the past two hours. She stared at him with huge eyes, her face paper-white.

"Sara?" His brows drew together as he took in her appearance.

"Oh, Matt!"

He stepped inside and shut the door. "Sara, sweetheart." He gripped her slender shoulders. "You're trembling. What the hell—"

"You've got to get out of here," she broke in.

"I've got to *what?*"

"You've got to get out of here!" she repeated. "He knows you're living here. You have to leave now, before he comes back."

"He who?"

"Santini!"

"Santini came here?"

"Yes! Only two hours ago. That man, Tank, was right, Matt. He knows. Santini *knows* about the money!"

"Sara—"

"You've got to get away!"

"Sara!" Matt shook her. "For godsake, what did Santini say to you?"

"He said I should tell you he knows about the money. Then he said to remind you he's part-Sicilian. Matt, this man is a lieutenant with the New York City Police Department!"

"I know who and what Joe Santini is."

"Then why are you acting this way? I lied to him! I lied to a *police officer!* I told him you were out of town and I didn't know where you were or when you were coming back. I was going to say I'd never heard of Matt Michaels, but he knew Dingbat, so I couldn't—oh, please, Matt, you've got to go." She swallowed convulsively, blinking back the tears she felt welling up. She looked down at the floor, fighting an overwhelming sense of weakness. "You've got to get away."

"Sara..." Matt's voice was very gentle. "Just what is it you think I've done?"

"I don't know." She *didn't* know. She had some suspicions, but she didn't know. "I...don't care." The last two words didn't come out very steadily, but she knew they were the truth as soon as they left her mouth.

"You lied to the police. That makes you an accessory after the fact, you know. Did you consider that?"

Sara's head came up, her lips parting to voice a protest. What she saw in Matt's brilliant blue eyes made the words die in her throat. He was gazing at her not with the anxiety she expected, but with an amused tenderness that made her heart turn over.

"Did you consider that?" he repeated.

Of course not. She'd been concentrating on him—to the exclusion of nearly everything else—ever since Lieutenant Joseph Santini knocked on the door.

Sara shook her head, thoroughly bewildered by the look in his eyes. Without quite registering what was going on, she let Matt shepherd her out of the foyer and into the living room. She heard him tell Dingbat to stay as he settled her on the couch. He took off his coat and sat down next to her.

"Sara, I don't know what kind of lurid scenarios you've been brewing in that beautiful red head of yours, but I am *not* a criminal. Oh, I may have a few unpaid parking tickets stuffed into my glove compartment, but Lieutenant Santini stopped bothering with misdemeanors like that when he graduated from walking a beat eighteen years ago."

"Then why—"

"Then why is he after me? His wife, Barbara, had a serious accident about six months ago. For various reasons too complex to go into, she was not covered by medical insurance at the time. Needless to say the bills were ferocious, and I heard the lieutenant was having trouble meeting them. So I arranged to help out."

"You paid his wife's medical bills?" Sara said in a stunned voice. She couldn't disguise her bewilderment.

Matt nodded, his lips quirking wryly at her reaction. "It was supposed to be kept quiet—an anonymous-benefactor sort of thing. Unfortunately, as Tank said the other day, somebody spilled at least some of the beans . . . and the lieutenant is a pro at uncovering the truth."

"You paid his wife's—" Sara knew she probably
sounded like a broken record. Then something in what
he'd just said triggered another question. "Who's Tank
Petrie?"

"Detective Sherman Petrie. NYPD."

"He's a policeman? But he looks and sounds like
a—"

"—a goon who breaks people's kneecaps?" he finished.

"Don't laugh at me!" She felt like Alice Through the
Looking Glass.

He took her hands. "I'm not laughing at you, sweetheart. Tank would be the first to admit he doesn't fit the
image of a cop. That's one reason he's so good at his
job."

"But what was all that about his being 'inside' and
then 'back on the streets?'" Sara demanded. He was
stroking the backs of her hands with his thumbs. The
caressing contact added to the confusing stew of emotions
stirring up within her.

"Some idiot got the stupid idea that Tank should be
slotted into a desk job. It apparently took him a few
months to convince the powers that be that it wasn't
going to work out."

"The . . . adjustment problem?" she asked slowly, putting the pieces together and not quite believing what she
got.

"That's right. I would have dearly loved to see Tank
exhibiting a bad attitude."

"And by 'back on the streets'—"

"He works plainclothes and undercover. There's a
special organized crime task force being formed and I've
got a hunch he's tied up with it. That's what he meant
about being low profile. That's also why I didn't explain
about him afterward. Although, God, Sara, if I'd realized
what you were thinking—"

"Why should Lieutenant Santini be angry about your paying those medical bills?" she asked abruptly. "It seems to me he should be grateful—"

"He's a very proud man and he doesn't like taking favors from anybody. He believes in taking care of his own. By the way, I'm pretty sure that's what he meant when he told you to remind me he's part-Sicilian." He paused. "I suppose you thought that was a reference to the Mafia."

For a man who had claimed not to know what was going on inside her head, he was embarrassingly perceptive.

She bit her lip, trying to assimilate the facts that Matt was laying out for her.

"I—if you—" she began awkwardly. "Where . . . where did you get the money to pay Lieutenant Santini's wife's medical bills?"

Sara felt a renewed sense of anxiety as his mouth settled into a grim line and a troubling shadow clouded his eyes. She didn't know what she would do if he lied to her.

"Sara, I haven't been dishonest with you about anything," he said slowly. "But I haven't really been honest, either. I hope you're going to be able to forgive me, because I realize now that you're a lady who needs the truth . . . who deserves it. Have you ever heard the name Mike Mathis?"

"Mike Mathis?" she echoed, looking at him blankly. Then, gradually, her expression changed. "The—the novelist?"

He nodded, saying nothing.

Yes. She'd heard the name—and had seen it emblazoned on rows of book covers as well. Mike Mathis was a writer of best-selling action novels. While Sara had never read any of them, she knew they were popular for their tautly realistic plots, their vividly drawn characters, and their liberal lacings of violence and steamy sex.

"You—you're Mike Mathis?"

"Or Mike Mathis is me. After ten years there are times when I'm not quite sure."

"But—but why didn't you just tell me? I asked you what you did—"

"I know, Sara. And believe me, I wish I had told you."

"Were you afraid I'd reveal your real name to *The New York Times*'s book critic?"

"No, of course not." He dismissed the idea with an abrupt gesture. "Considering the amount of publicity I did for my last book my identity is hardly veiled in mystery."

"Then why wouldn't you...Matt, did you think I was asking questions out of idle curiosity? It was...it *is* important to me to know you. To *really* know you."

"Sara—"

"Are you ashamed of the sort of books you write?" She was searching desperately for an explanation.

"No!" he replied sharply, his tone giving her the impression that she had unwittingly touched a nerve. He released her hands, then raked his fingers back through his ebony hair in a restless gesture. "Although my family is."

"They are?"

"Perhaps *embarrassed* is a better word," he amended.

"But why? Most people would be thrilled to have a successful author in their family."

His sensual mouth curved into a mocking smile. "Ah, but as my mother and stepfather would no doubt point out, they are not 'most people.' Now, if I'd written a brain-numbing esoteric tome that sold a dozen copies and was condescendingly termed 'promising' by some pretentiously obscure literary supplement, they probably would have forgiven me my many social sins—or at least graciously overlooked them on the grounds of artistic eccentricity. But, no. Somehow I had the dumb luck to write a novel that was very successful. Too successful to qualify for the snob-appeal sweepstakes."

He paused for a moment, giving a small, mirthless laugh.

"It probably didn't help the situation that one of the villains in my first novel bore a very nasty—a close to libelous—resemblance to my stepfather. Looking back, it was a stupid thing to do, but I was still suffering from the after-effects of a long-term case of adolescent rebellion when I wrote the book."

"You thought I'd react the way your family has if you told me about your writing?" Sara knew she was conservative and cautious in her values, but it hurt to think that Matt might have classed her with a group of people he obviously disdained.

He reached forward and ran one finger very lightly down her cheek.

"No, not at all. How could I think that about a woman who takes on unknown intruders with a squash racquet? Or who attacks men with alligators in the middle of F.A.O. Schwarz?"

The look of melting tenderness was back in his eyes, but it could not dispel her deep-seated insecurities. Only his honesty could do that.

"If that's true, Matt, *why didn't you tell me?*"

He sighed. "It wasn't any one reason, Sara. I suppose it's because I've got some pretty . . . mixed-up . . . feelings about a lot of things in my life, including my alter ego, Mike Mathis. You've never read any of his—my—stuff, have you?"

She shook her head once. "I'm sorry."

"Don't apologize. Anyway, in the beginning, I—ah—didn't handle my success too well. I was just twenty-four when the first book came out, and I wasn't the most emotionally mature person in the world. I'd raised a lot of hell as a kid, especially after my father died and my mother remarried, but all of a sudden I was running with a crowd who made a profession out of living in the fast lane. To make a long and messy story short, I developed a problem drawing a line between Mathieson Michaels and Mike Mathis."

Sara's memory was feeding back bits of magazine articles she'd read about "Mike Mathis." She frowned, trying to put them together with what Matt was telling her.

"You—your first book was somewhat autobiographical, wasn't it?" she asked.

"A writer has to write about what he knows, Sara. When I started out, one of the few things I knew anything about was myself. So, yes, I stuck quite a few pieces of 'me' into the first book, and into the next two as well. I embroidered and imagined a lot, too. But that didn't seem to matter after a while. I got caught up in this 'Mike Mathis' persona without realizing it. I think the rude awakening came when I realized that people were getting turned on by their fantasies about him without giving the slightest damn about who I really was."

"For 'people' should I read 'women?'" Sara questioned softly.

"Yeah," he acknowledged. "In any case, I eventually managed to get my head screwed on straight. I did a lot of traveling, which gave me plenty of exotic scenery to use in my books. I came to New York about two years ago to do some research for a novel about the police department."

"That's how you got to know Lieutenant Santini and Detective Petrie?"

"Umm-hmm. Then I made the big mistake of going out to Hollywood to work on a screen treatment of one of my books. All of a sudden I was back to being 'Mike Mathis, best-selling author' again. I ended up loading Ding, some clothes, and a few boxes of stuff into my car and taking off on a six-month cross-country trip."

"Which brought you back to New York."

"Which brought me back to New York," he agreed. "Where, very early one fateful Monday morning, I let myself into an apartment I thought was empty and found you."

"A 'squash-racquet-wielding female in a see-through nightgown,'" she quoted.

His mouth quirked. "Oh, I found much more than that. I found a natural redhead who didn't know Mike Mathis from a hole in the ground, but who seemed to be willing to...tolerate...Matt Michaels after she got over the belief that he was a would-be rapist or burglar, and before she started suspecting him of being on the lam from a part-Sicilian police lieutenant."

Sara's tongue darted out to moisten her lips. She saw a flare of response in Matt's cobalt eyes. Her heart was thudding in a syncopated rhythm.

"I—I had some very good reasons for my suspicions, Matt," she said in breathless defense. She was a captive of his slowly heating gaze.

"I know you did." There was an odd note in the way he said this.

"You must think I'm a fool," she murmured, hearing the edge in his voice.

He reached out to stroke his fingertips over the curve of her cheek. He traced teasingly down the line of her nose, then slowly marked the shape of her mouth. The soft pink flesh of her lower lip tingled from his touch.

"No," he told her, bringing his other hand up to cradle the side of her head. His lean fingers threaded through the soft tangle of her freshly washed auburn hair. "I don't think you're a fool."

Her lips parted of their own volition as he drew her to him with an erotic deliberation. He did not hurry her...or himself. There was no need to rush toward a conclusion they both recognized as inevitable.

This is what we both want, his eyes seemed to be telling her. Let's savor every moment of it.

Matt did not take the kiss when he finally bent his head and found her mouth; Sara gave it eagerly. She opened to him willingly, not simply accepting his deepening of the caress, but inviting the intimate exploration of his tongue with a tantalizing movement of her own.

He'd tasted of anger and pent-up passion the night they'd kissed and then quarreled. There was no anger in him now, although Sara sensed he was holding his desires in check. She could feel the tension building in his lithe body as she arched against him.

She brought her arms up his back, her palms learning the leanly muscled contours beneath the smooth cotton of his shirt. Locking her hands behind his neck, she ran her fingers into the luxurious thickness of his night-dark hair.

It was not simple physical need that set her pulse pounding and ignited the tiny flames licking along her skin. There had been an insistent sexual awareness between them from the very first, but it went beyond mere attraction. The emptiness Sara had begun experiencing when Matt was not near; the blossoming completeness she felt herself moving toward now—he had become a part of her.

One of his hands glided up her back, stroking the line of her spine through the thin fabric of her tank top. She shivered pleasurably as he reached the point where the material ended and the soft, sensitive skin of her upper back and shoulders was left bare for his touch.

His scent was intoxicating and evocatively unique. She was conscious of the faint but fresh astringency of his after shave and of the underlying muskiness of his maleness. Eyes closed, but with her other senses tuned to a quivering pitch, she nuzzled her lips against his neck, nipping once with her teeth.

She felt rather than heard the sound of the response he gave.

"Tank didn't know the half of it when he said I was

distracted the other day," he murmured into her ear. "Obsessed would have been closer to the mark. God, Sara, do you know how much I've wanted—needed— to touch you? The feel of you in my arms is so *right,* sweetheart."

"Mmmm. . . .Matt—"

He sought her mouth again. This time the kiss was hungrier, less studied. The demanding contact sent a thrill of excitement racing along Sara's body and she shifted instinctively, wanting to press against him more intimately.

Then, unbelievably, he began to withdraw. It was not at all rejection: There was too much reluctance in the way he pulled back for that. Even as he lifted his head, his arms remained around her, holding her possessively.

Sara opened her eyes, her expression bemused. "Matt?" she whispered huskily.

"I have to know something before we go any further," he said unsteadily.

She gave a low, delicious laugh, her wide gray-green eyes glowing with promise and provocation. "Whatever it is," she replied, "the answer is *yes*."

His own eyes were alight with a sapphire blaze, but he shook his head once, his features going taut with determination.

"I want to make love with you, Sara," he told her. "But first you have to tell me why you lied for me when you didn't for Gary Beaumont."

Chapter 6

"H-HOW DO YOU know about Gary?" Sara asked in an appalled voice, the color draining out of her face. She tried to break free of his embrace. Matt held her firmly but gently, his eyes telling her that he would not let her escape—or push him away.

"Your sister called earlier today."

"My sister!"

"She wanted to talk. To me."

"But why?"

"Would you believe she was worried about you?"

"Chrissie?" She didn't even try to hide her disbelief. Her sister, in her blithe-butterfly selfishness, seldom worried about anyone but herself.

Just like Gary. Sara shuddered involuntarily. Matt's arms tightened protectively.

"From the little I know about Chrissie, I gather she deserves that kind of skeptical reaction," he said quietly.

"But she was worried about you when she called—in an indirect sort of way."

"What does that mean?" Sara demanded.

"She found out who I was."

"I don't—" she began bewilderedly, then stopped as she suddenly realized what he meant. The color that had left her cheeks surged back into them in a rush of hot blood. "You mean she found out you're Mike Mathis."

"Umm-hmm. And I think she likes the idea of your living with a best-selling author better than the thought of your shacking up with a family disgrace who puts up bail for his low-life connections."

"She said that?" Her eyes widened in shock.

"She was just quoting Lowell. And frankly, I'd rather she quoted him to me than to you. By the way, the bail money he was upset about on that particular occasion was bail I put up for a bunch of environmental activists. They'd been arrested for protesting on the grounds of a chemical factory Lowell's father owns."

"Oh."

"In any case, once Chrissie got through dropping some very unsubtle hints about what Mike Mathis could do for her, we had a very interesting discussion about you . . . and Gary Beaumont."

"Matt, I don't want to—" She was trembling.

"—talk about him? I realize that, Sara, but it's important for both our sakes that you do."

"What happened with Gary is the past. It's over."

"It's not over until you put it behind you, sweetheart. And you haven't. Because of this creep Beaumont and your philandering father, you've convinced yourself that no man can be trusted. You've been hurt twice and you don't want to be hurt again, so you're suspicious. That's natural—it's human. It's also a hell of a way to go through life."

Sara swallowed convulsively. "What did—what did Chrissie tell you?"

"I'd rather hear it from you."

She took a deep breath, expelling it slowly. Looking into his steady blue eyes, she realized she had to tell him the truth. It was, as he had said, important to both of them that she did. But she was still so ashamed.

He divined her thoughts with disconcerting accuracy. "Sara, if someone deliberately uses you or lies to you, he's the one who should be ashamed," he declared quietly.

"All right. I'll tell you," she said finally. "My parents didn't have a happy marriage. I think my father was unfaithful from the very first. He never had a lot of time for us—my mother, Chrissie, me. I remember he used to promise he'd come to open house at school on parents' day or to see Chrissie in a play, but he never did. I—I asked my mother how he could be such a liar, and she said that's the way men are. She said the same thing when he left her for the first time to m-move in with one of his girl friends. She also said that a woman just had to accept it."

Sara paused here, trying to sort through the memories and put the right words together. Matt said nothing, but she could feel the support in his touch. Sighing, she went on.

"I decided that if that was true, I wasn't going to get involved with any man . . . *ever*. And I didn't, until Gary. A few years after I graduated from college I got a job with the accounting department of a large company in Syracuse. Chrissie had moved to Manhattan to study acting and my mother was on the verge of remarrying, so I felt—oh, I don't know exactly—"

"Free?"

"Freer," she amended. "About a year after I went to work at the company, Gary arrived. He was related to the chairman of the board somehow. He also projected this incredible aura of charm and confidence. Every woman in the place was crazy about him."

"Including you?"

"Including me," she acknowledged flatly. "Six months or so after he got there he asked me out. I don't know who was more shocked, me, or the rest of the female employees. We dated, very casually at first, then more and more frequently. He—we—talked about marriage. I thought I was in love with him."

She bit her lip, almost welcoming the painful dig of her teeth. It was nothing compared to the agony she had known because of Gary.

"About the time our relationship turned serious I discovered some discrepancies in the company's books. It was nothing alarming, just unexplained deviations from regular accounting practices. At first I thought it might have something to do with the fact that we were in the middle of switching over to a new computer system. But the problem persisted. I—I did some checking. Finally, it became clear that all the irregularities could be traced back to Gary in some way. Everything pointed to the idea that he was stealing from the firm."

"But you had trouble accepting the possibility that he was guilty of that," Matt filled in.

She nodded. "I—I went to him with the evidence I had. I wanted to believe I'd made some mistake, that there was some *explanation*. At first he tried to dismiss it. Then he stopped denying it and said he needed the money so we could be m-married. He...he wanted me to h-help him to cover everything up." Her hazel eyes were full of anguish. "He said if I really loved him, I'd do it. *If I really loved him*."

"Sara—"

"When I finally pulled myself together enough to say no, he turned abusive. He threatened to implicate me if I said anything to anyone. And he told me that the o-only reason he'd bothered with me in the first place was that he'd thought I'd be useful."

There was a long silence. Matt broke it with one

lethally spoken epithet, then asked, "What happened?"

"I went to the chairman of the board. He was an honorable man and he believed what I told him, even though Gary tried to...to..." Her voice trailed off. "Despite the fact that I hadn't acted properly when I initially found the irregularities, the board made it clear that they wanted me to stay with the company. The situation was hushed up, but Gary was forced to resign. I kept my position for about nine months, then took a leave of absence. While I was trying to decide what to do next I was offered a job with an accounting firm in Manhattan. I think the chairman helped arrange it, but I'm not certain. In any case, I took it."

"What about Beaumont?" There was a dangerous edge to the inquiry.

"I don't know where he is. I heard he married some wealthy older woman and went to Europe with her. I— I don't care. Not anymore."

She closed her eyes for a moment, a curious wave of relief washing over her. Usually, she tried to avoid thinking, much less speaking in detail, about Gary. Opening her eyes, she was aware of a strange sense of liberation. It was as though she'd exorcised the poisonous doubts and insecurities that had been eating away at her for so long.

"But you did care at the time he asked you to lie for him," Matt stated very carefully. His face had gone as hard and as unreadable as a graven mask.

They were back to his original question. Sara's heart began to pound. She knew—she'd known from the start— what he was really asking. The thought of answering terrified her. How could she admit to him what she hadn't been able to admit to herself?

"I c-cared—"

"But you didn't lie."

"Matt—"

"You lied for me, Sara. Suspecting—no, *believing*

me guilty of God knows what, you lied to the police for me."

"Please—"

"Why?"

"I just did it. I don't know why!" She could feel her pulse beating wildly, throbbing in her temples. Try as she would, she couldn't look away from his demanding cobalt stare. He seemed to be X-raying her very soul, searing away the protective layers, the defensive barriers, to leave her emotionally naked and vulnerable.

"I think you do know." His tone was implacable.

She broke against his resolution. "What do you want me to say?" she demanded raggedly. "That I lied because I care about you more than I cared about Gary? That I lied because I—I'm in love with you?" Her voice cracked. "Is that what you want to hear?"

The change in his face was like the night giving way to dawn. The grim determination melted into a glorious tenderness.

"I hope it's what you want to hear, too," he said huskily.

Her lips parted. "Matt—?" she breathed wonderingly.

"I'm in love with you, Sara," he told her simply.

She swallowed. "You—you don't have to say that," she whispered, trembling. She wanted desperately to believe him, but she'd learned, through bitter, wounding experience that the word *love* was often attached to the worst lies of all.

"Yes, I do," he assured her, and gathering her close once again, he bent his head and kissed her.

Afterward Sara had no clear memory of how they got from the living room into her bedroom. She could recall fragments—the feeling of being lifted up and carried, the sound of his heel nudging the door shut, the soft flare of the bedside light being turned on—but that was all. His kiss held her in thrall.

Reality, blissful and breathtaking, began as he laid her down on the bed and stretched out next to her, the mattress giving slightly under his greater weight.

A soft flush of excitement mantled her creamy cheeks and a provocative smokiness appeared in her wide eyes as she gazed up at him. She lifted one hand and ran her fingers down his face, following the lean strength of his cheek and jaw, then lightly stroked the lines of his sensual mouth. He nipped playfully at her fingertip, nibbling at the tender flesh as though tasting a rare and delicious delicacy.

This time she initiated the kiss. They explored each other's mouths hungrily, arousingly. Teasing, torment-ing, lingering, their tongues and lips moved in heady, instinctive rhythm. She made a soft whimpering sound as he laved the velvety flesh inside her lower lip, then thrust deeply into the sweet recesses of her mouth.

"I've been dreaming about this for so long, Sara," he murmured, kissing his way down the smooth length of her neck and nuzzling erotically against the hollow at the base of her throat. "If I'm still dreaming, don't wake me up—ever."

"I won't," she promised unsteadily. "Ah—"

A gentle tug pulled her tank top free from the waist-band of her shorts. She arched, quivering as he slipped one hand beneath the thin cloth, stroking her naked skin. The lower half of her body had turned to a fiery jelly. Her own hands moved to the buttons of his shirt. One by one the small fasteners gave way to her trembling fingers.

He paused long enough to shrug out of the shirt, discarding it carelessly. The smile he turned on her had the freebooter's flash she had seen before. Her eyes trav-eled downward in a sweep, taking in the lean breadth of his torso, the half-hidden circles of his nipples, and the triangle of his dark chest hair.

He was still smiling when she returned her scrutiny

to his face, the molten blue of his eyes darkening with desire to a deep midnight hue.

"My turn to look at you, sweetheart."

A moment later she was naked from the waist up, her tank top joining his shirt somewhere on the floor.

"I've been dreaming about this, too," he told her. "But for once my imagination wasn't up to the reality. You're beautiful, Sara."

Gently, he cupped each breast, his palm warm and possessive as it curved over the softly swelling flesh. He circled each nipple with the ball of his thumb, sending lightning flashes of pleasure coursing through her as the pink peaks stiffened from rose-petal softness to a yearning tautness.

"M-Matt, please—" she moaned.

He kissed one of the flower-tipped globes, his tongue flicking lightly back and forth until she moaned out his name again. Taking the hardened nipple into his mouth, he sucked for what seemed to be an endless moment of almost painful delight. His heated breath fanned across her sensitized skin as he transferred his expert attentions to her other breast.

She slipped her arms around him, her hands gliding up his back, savoring the responsive movement of muscle, the warm pliancy of skin, even the unmistakable but mysterious ridging of his scars. She pressed her mouth against the smooth strength of one of his shoulders, tasting the faint tang of his perspiration.

Their legs were tangled together, making her feverishly aware of the thrusting demand of his desire. She stroked her palms wantonly over the taut contours of his denim-covered buttocks, a thrill of intensely female satisfaction lancing through her when he shuddered and lifted his head.

"Sara—" His voice was thick.

"Please—" she said urgently. "I want you *now*, Matt."

He was up, out of his jeans, and back beside her in

little longer than a heartbeat. Her brain recorded her first glimpse of his superb male nudity in a flash of unbearable excitement. The twin images of lithe symmetry and un-ashamed arousal burned themselves indelibly into her memory.

He undid the catch at the waistband of her shorts, then unzipped the front. She wriggled, lifting her hips as he tugged the brief garment downward along with her ecru lace panties.

And then they were naked together, bound by the most complex of emotions and the most basic of needs. Each breath, each touch, each burning kiss, was designed to pleasure . . . and to provoke.

Their lips met in passionate fusion, seeking hungrily. One of Matt's hands was cradling Sara's head while the other moved down the length of her body to search out her secrets. He brought her once, twice, to the verge of fulfillment, leading her to the edge, then coaxing her back, urging her to a higher plateau of passion.

Finally, he moved up and over her and they went over the edge, consumed in the fires of their own making. It was far more than mutual giving and receiving. It was completion.

Reborn, Sara thought dazedly. *That's how I feel, re-born*.

Her head was resting against Matt's chest and the rest of her body was curved against him in seductive vul-nerability. She could hear his heart beating and feel the slow rise and fall of his breathing. Gently, with uncon-scious possessiveness, she trailed her fingertips up his torso, teasing over the crisp mat of dark hair.

Matt caught her hand, pressing it flat with one palm. His other palm was fitted to the yielding line of her slender waist.

"I'm afraid this is going to get you kicked out of the AICPA," he commented lazily, shifting himself slightly and dropping a kiss on her temple.

"Hmmm?" she breathed dreamily. "What does the American Institute of Certified Public Accountants have to do with anything?"

"Well, unless I am greatly mistaken about what just happened between us, you're in serious violation of that chastity clause you told me about two weeks ago."

"Chast—oh, that." She laughed, remembering the scene in the lobby.

"They'll probably strip you of your green eyeshade," he went on.

"There's not much else to strip me of," she agreed unsteadily.

"Especially when they find out you're in violation with a man who hasn't balanced his checkbook in the last, oh, two years or so," he added.

Sara lifted her head. "You must be joking!"

"Nope. I never was very good with numbers. Of course, I'm terrific at handling figures—"

"M-Matt!" His name came out in a gasp of pleasure.

"Just doing a quick inventory of some fixed assets," he informed her outrageously, withdrawing his hand. His eyes were alight with laughter and a kind of wondering passion. He eased away from her slightly, propping himself up on one elbow.

She smiled up at him, her auburn curls spilling around her head like a silken sunburst. Her fresh complexion had a new glow to it and her mouth curved, rosy-ripe, into a smile of alluring invitation.

"Fixed assets, hmmm?" she returned. "Well, I hope you remember to make allowances for depreciation."

He chuckled, dipping his head to kiss the tip of her nose. "Sara, sweetheart, what you have doesn't depreciate. It just gets better with time—much better."

"Matt . . ." Sara said suddenly. "What about Lieutenant Santini?"

"We'll work something out," he replied casually.

"Do you—do you think he knew I was lying to him?"

"Probably. But don't worry, you can plead temporary insanity when they come to haul you away on obstruction-of-justice charges."

"Very funny!" she retorted. "On the other hand, if I get sent to prison, I won't have to worry about finding a place to stay."

"Sara—"

"Well, your stepbrother is coming back from Switzerland eventually." She sighed. "So I'll need a new apartment."

"Yes, but we don't have to start looking for one tonight, do we?"

He placed a slight but unmistakable emphasis on the word *we*. Sara's heart performed a curious tap dance when she heard it.

"No," she murmured. "We don't."

He stroked his fingers through her hair. "I am sorry you had to handle Santini all by yourself."

"Where—where were you tonight?"

"I had an appointment with Lydia Follett."

Sara went very still, hating the cold chill of suspicion that settled over her. She fought to keep her face from revealing the sudden surge of turmoil inside her. The change in Matt's expression told her she was not successful.

"Sara," he said slowly. "Sara, I understand that we still don't know each other all that well, and that you're a little scared of me. Sweetheart, I'm a little scared of you, too. But you're going to have to try to let go of the fear and trust me. I realize that trusting doesn't come easily to you."

"I trust you," she protested, sitting up and drawing the bedclothes around her. "I lied for you . . . made love with—"

He sat up, too, his expression grave yet deeply compassionate. He cupped her face in both hands, hushing her with a shake of his head.

"It wasn't trust that made you lie to Santini," he said gently. "And as for making love with me—"

Sara was trembling. "I'm sorry," she whispered. She hadn't been reborn at all. She'd only been briefly released from the corrosive doubts that were the legacy of her experiences with her father and Gary Beaumont.

Matt gathered her against him, her yielding breasts pressing against the strength of his chest. "Don't be sorry. I haven't given you a whole hell of a lot of reason to trust me over the past two weeks. That's why I left you the note saying we had to talk. God, when I got through with Chrissie this afternoon, I finally began to realize what's been going through your head. I was playing it cagey because of my hangups, and you were backing off because every move I made seemed to confirm your worst suspicions."

"Not quite every move."

"Okay, every other one." His breath ruffled her hair and she nestled against him. They were silent for a few seconds. "I meant it when I said I wouldn't hurt you, Sara," he told her. "And Lydia Follett is my literary agent, not my lover."

She pulled away from him a little, genuinely taken aback by this statement.

"That *was* what you thought when you saw her leaving the apartment, wasn't it?" he teased. "And you *were* jealous."

She flushed hotly, veiling her eyes with her lashes. "Sort of," she mumbled, feeling utterly foolish.

"You sort of thought we were lovers or you were sort of jealous?"

"I was jealous," she admitted. "And I thought you and Lydia were ... lovers. Sort of."

"What does that mean?"

"It's just that you were so evasive about what you did for a living. At first I thought you might be unemployed and embarrassed about it . . . or on vacation or something. But you had so much money and—and—"

"No visible means of support?" he interpolated.

"Then when I came home that day and found Lydia, and you and she were obviously, you know . . . I mean, I thought you had been—except she said it was strictly business—" Mortified and miserable, she finally looked up at him. "And then she said the afternoon had been tantalizing and you said she was insatiable—" She couldn't go on.

"Are you trying to say that you thought I was her paid—ah—stud?" He made the inquiry in the politest of tones. Although his face was schooled to unreadability, he could not tamp down the alarming blaze in his eyes.

Sara nodded once, bracing herself for his anger, his contempt, his rejection.

His mouth started to twitch. Then his shoulders started to shake. All at once he erupted with laughter, collapsing helplessly back onto the pillows. "And . . . and . . . I suppose when she . . . she mentioned giving my name to some . . . somebody else . . ." he gasped out.

"Well, she did say this person was willing to pay you lots of money for what you like to do best," Sara defended herself, clutching the coverlet even more tightly about her body.

"Oh, Sara, Sara, you may be a CPA, but you've got an imagination that should be banned in Boston. A gigolo, huh?" Grinning boldly, he reached up and pulled her abruptly on top of him. "Tell me, sweetheart, having sampled the service, do you still think I could make a living at loving?"

"M-Matt—" Despite herself, she was starting to laugh, too. "I don't—ah! *Oh!*"

Before she realized his intention, he'd shifted his weight

and flipped her over onto her back, his knee riding firmly between her thighs, his hands pinning her wrists against the bed.

"What?" he asked, swooping down to snatch a quick kiss. "You say you haven't had sufficient opportunity to make a final assessment?"

"Matt!" She wriggled in a movement that was more voluptuous than protesting. "What are you do—ooh!"

"This, love, is what is known as appreciation of assets."

Sara had seldom truly slept with a man. While she and Gary had been lovers, he had spent the entire night with her only rarely. In the acrimony of their final confrontation, he'd made it cruelly and explicitly clear that there were times when, having left her arms, he'd sought satisfaction with more experienced company.

Now, with the bliss of the previous night hazing her brain like incense, Sara awoke to the knowledge of what it was like to truly share a bed with a man. She discovered that the idea of it was flavored with a uniquely intimate sensuality.

They'd been curved together in sleep, with Sara's backside fitted against Matt's front while one of his arms held her close. She lay there for a few moments, savoring the feel of his embrace, the sensation of naked skin against naked skin.

Stifling a yawn, she shifted away slowly, disengaging herself from his hold with genuine reluctance. He made an inarticulate sound low in his throat, and rolled over onto his stomach.

Sara glanced over at the bedside clock, breathing a silent prayer of relief when she saw that it was only a few minutes past six. Under normal circumstances she didn't get out of bed until six-thirty on a work day.

Of course, these were hardly normal circumstances . . .

She was going to get up—eventually. And she was going to go to work. But right now, in this quiet morning peace, she wanted to feast her eyes on the man sleeping next to her.

His ebony hair was more mussed than ever, and his strong features were relaxed into something very near vulnerability. Sara placed a butterfly-light kiss on the tanned plane of one of his cheeks, holding her breath as the dark crescents of his thick lashes seemed to flutter.

He did not wake up. She vacillated briefly between relief and disappointment, then continued with her scrutiny.

Quite naturally, her gaze lingered on the bronzed expanse of his back—and on the scars that marred it. She had not lied to him about her reaction the morning she had first seen the marks. She *had* been surprised, but that had passed.

Gently . . . very gently . . . she followed the smooth power of his shoulders with the tip of one finger. She circled his right shoulder blade and then his left with the concentration of a professional figure skater.

Lulled by the continued evenness of his slow, deep breathing, she kissed the back of his neck, her chestnut curls mingling with his own night-dark thatch. Then, her expression oddly intent, she began to trace the length of his scars with her soft, moist lips.

Kiss and make it better, a small voice murmured in her head. Matt had expected her to be revolted by the marks—or, at least, he had been prepared for the possibility. Perhaps the injury didn't hurt anymore *physically* . . . but some psychological pain obviously remained.

There was a small, downy patch of hair at the base of his spine, right below the spot where his scars ended. It was fine as dandelion fuzz, and Sara blew on it experimentally.

"Sara, for godsake, a simple good morning would do," Matt's voice informed her thickly.

Thoroughly startled, she gave a surprised yelp and froze. A second later he rolled over and sat up. Whether by accident or design, a twist of sheet modestly covered him from waist to mid-thigh.

"You—you're awake!" she accused him, scrambling to sit up and cover up as well.

"Sweetheart, you could bring a dead man back to life with what you were doing."

"Then why didn't you say something?" She cleared her throat, wondering if her cheeks were as pink as they felt.

"Because I was curious to see how far you were going to go."

"Oh." She bit her lip. How far *would* she have gone? It struck her that she had absolutely no idea.

Sensible Sara . . . the sex maniac?

"We can continue with the experiment if you want," Matt told her with a rakish gleam in his eye. "I'm perfectly willing to go all the way."

"Mmmm." She made what she devotedly hoped was a neutral sound. "Are you—um—going running this morning?"

"Do you honestly think I'd have the energy?" he inquired silkily.

"We-e-ll—"

"Haven't you heard that runners have to remain celibate to sustain their strength?"

"That old wives' tale!"

"Old wives have been known to be right, Sara. I think I'd be hard pressed to roll out of bed after last night, much less go out running. Hell, you've probably ruined me for the Olympics, too." Grinning, he leaned forward and gave her a long, lingering kiss.

She emerged from the embrace breathless and more than a little aroused. "A simple good morning would do," she quoted back at him, squirming away as he slipped a searching hand underneath the sheets.

An oddly thoughtful look flickered through his eyes. "My back really doesn't bother you, does it?"

She ran her fingers through her hair, fluffing the curls experimentally. "The only thing that bothers me is that whatever happened to put the scars there must have been awful," she said seriously.

He seemed to hesitate for a moment. "I—I dropped out of Yale near the end of my second semester after a major argument with my stepfather," he told her slowly. "He'd more or less mapped out my entire academic career and I'd more or less responded by telling him where he could stick his map. Anyway, I decided to assert my independence—or demonstrate my pigheadedness, depending on your perspective. So I quit school and enlisted in the army."

He paused, raking his hand back through his hair in an impatient gesture. "You think Tank Petrie looks tough? You should have seen the drill instructor in charge of my platoon in basic training. The amazing thing is, I took to the military like the proverbial duck to water. Eventually, I wound up as part of a special counter-insurgency program and was sent overseas as a trainer. Unfortunately, some of the insurgents decided to counter my training—and me—with a fragmentation grenade."

"Oh, Matt!"

"Scratch one would-be hero." He shrugged ruefully. "I was flown back to the States to spend the next three months or so alternating between being bored out of my skull lying in a hospital bed and being manhandled by a three-hundred-pound physical therapist named Elmo who'd obviously studied under the Marquis de Sade at some point in his career. Not that he wasn't good at his job—quite the opposite, in fact. But that didn't keep me from fantasizing about what I'd do to him once I recovered. I started writing down some of my revenge scenarios. There wasn't much else to do. Then, one day after he got done beating up on my trapezius for the day,

I let Elmo read a few pages. For some reason he thought they were great. He said with my imagination I should write a book."

"And you did."

"Yeah. I wrote my way through about a dozen legal pads before I was discharged. In the meantime, I also established a truce of sorts with my family, so I went home to finish my recuperation by spending the summer lolling around the country club swimming pool and polishing my—ah—masterpiece. The trouble was, my back tended to put the local gentry off their gin and tonics. My mother, in particular, was offended. She wasn't too thrilled when she got a look at what I was writing, either. But then, she didn't like what she read when I was a kid and she sneaked a peek into my secret journal."

"What . . . what finally happened?"

"I came to New York. I started peddling my manuscript around and eventually hooked up with Lydia who, incidentally, was as rough on me in her own fashion as Elmo was in his. In the end, my book got published and Mike Mathis was born—scars and all." His voice held an odd combination of pride and irony.

"Why did you use a pen name?"

"A combination of reasons. Protective coloration, in a way. To keep some semblance of peace with my family. And, I suppose, because I had this . . . I don't know . . . hope, I guess, that someday I'd write something I'd want to put my real name to." His eyes were pensive.

"Did you—did you send Elmo a complimentary copy of your first book?" she questioned, wanting to ease the hurt she felt in him.

Her inquiry had the desired effect. Matt grinned, his memory-shadowed mood lightening. "I dedicated the damn thing to him," he said. "It seemed only fair, considering that he was the one who inspired the fantasies that got my literary juices flowing . . . so to speak."

"It was the least you could do," she agreed solemnly,

not missing the sudden glint in his eye.

"And speaking of fantasies..." he drawled meaningfully.

"Matt, I've got to get up and take a shower," she protested.

"Great." He flung off the sheet in a sweeping movement. "Showers have always had a special place in my fantasies."

Chapter 7

SARAH DECIDED THAT showers were going to have a special place in her fantasies, too.

Although she left the apartment a bit behind schedule, she managed to arrive at the office a few minutes early thanks to a cabbie whose own fantasies apparently involved kamikaze raids and demolition derbies. Normally, the man's hair-raising traffic tactics would have left Sara looking as green as the celadon silk shirtwaist she was wearing. On this particular morning, however, she remained blissfully oblivious to everything but her own very pleasant thoughts.

She spent the bulk of her morning engrossed in preliminary work on the firm's latest consulting contract. It involved a New Jersey electronics firm that was trying to handle the pressures of an unprecedented—and somewhat unexpected—period of expansion. Sara was one of a team of accountants who would be working to come up with recommendations to insure that the company became better as it became bigger.

The consulting team was headed by Bryce Warren, one of her firm's senior partners. He was a slight, silver-haired man in his early sixties, who regarded a properly prepared balance sheet with the passionate appreciation other people reserve for great works of art. Legend had it that he was capable of delivering an hour-long scholarly dissertation on the history of double-entry bookkeeping, tracing it back to its supposed inventor, an Italian monk in late medieval times.

"I understand you had the—ah—opportunity to deal with Mr. Thompson and his taxes yesterday, Miss Edwards," he commented with pleasant precision as the meeting on the consulting contract broke up.

"That's right, sir," Sara replied, neatly stacking the financial reports that had been given to her to review. Although the older man's mild features were schooled into an expression of courteous interest, she detected a slight gleam in his calm gray eyes. She recalled her suspicion the day before that the session with the semi-hysterical client had been some sort of a test. "It was . . . interesting."

The gleam brightened to an unmistakable sparkle. "Some of your colleagues have been less tactful in their descriptions of Mr. Thompson in the past," he observed with a small chuckle. "I realize tax accounting is not your area of specialty, but might I ask how you handled the situation?"

"Mr. Thompson's returns seemed perfectly straight-forward and in order, so I advised him of that," she replied, then smiled. "I also suggested he try having a stiff drink to relax him before we met for the audit."

Mr. Warren chuckled again. "I rather think you—and the poor unfortunate at the IRS who has to conduct Mr. Thompson's audit—will be the ones in need of the stiff drink," he responded. "Well, I look forward to working with you on this new consulting job, Miss Edwards."

"Thank you, Mr. Warren." With an inexplicable but pleasant feeling of having been given an official stamp of approval, Sara took her leave.

Once back in her small but neatly organized office, she decided to order lunch at her desk. A phone call to a nearby food-delivery service produced a fresh Greek salad brimming with crisp iceberg and romaine lettuce, marinated olives, tomatoes, onions, and chunks of tangy feta cheese. Sara ate the meal absently as she skimmed through the stack of financial information she had been given. She paused from time to time to jot down a note or to underline something.

She also found her mind drifting inevitably back over the events of the past twenty-four hours.

She was in love with Mathieson Michaels. She wasn't certain how or when it had happened, but she had fallen deeply in love with him. It was more than a matter of giving herself to him. The attraction—the awareness— she had felt for him from the first had taken root and blossomed long before she had yielded herself so willingly to his passionate lovemaking.

And Mathieson Michaels was in love with her . . . or so he said.

Sara froze a little inside as she realized she had tacked on the caveat without really thinking about it. Just adding such a qualifier cheapened what she and Matt had.

But what *did* they have?

Sara frowned, doodling several question marks in the margin of the annual report she was going through. She frowned more deeply when she saw what she had done.

What's wrong with me? she asked herself. If I let my life be ruled by doubts and questions, it won't be much of a life.

But on the other hand, she added, I can't just accept everything on blind faith . . .

Trust. Matt had been all too right when he'd said he knew it was something she did not do easily. Painful personal experience had made her wary—wary of caring, of letting her guard down, of allowing anyone to get close enough to hurt her.

Sara sighed. She *did* care. She *had* let down her guard and allowed someone to get close. And, in return, Matt had loved her, cherished her.

Trusted her?

The phone rang. She picked it up.

"Sara Edwards," she said.

"Mathieson Michaels."

Her heart skipped a beat. "Matt! I was just thinking about you."

"Ah, so you aren't getting any work done today, either." he returned with silken innuendo.

Her laugh was soft. "Well—"

"I miss you, sweetheart."

The words sent a thrill up her spine. She stroked the pale green skirt of her dress in unthinking sensuality, her fingers gliding lightly over the thin silk. "I've been gone for only five hours," she protested.

"Five hours and twenty minutes, but who's counting?"

"I miss you, too, Matt," she confessed.

"How's your day going?"

"Very well, actually. I think I passed some kind of firm initiation test. And I've been assigned to work on a new consulting project for a company in New Jersey. What about you?"

"Well, to tell the truth, I've been wallowing in the flow of literary juices all morning. You're one hell of an inspiration."

"Better than Elmo?" she teased.

"Hmmm..."

"Matt!"

"It's no contest. Elmo's a lot bigger than you, of course, but I've always been a firm believer in quality, not quantity."

"So, you're working on a new Mike Mathis book?"

"Mmm . . . not exactly. I've got a lot of things on my mind—new ideas, feelings. It helps to get them down on paper. By the way, I had a long friend-to-friend talk with Joe Santini this morning."

He doesn't want to talk about his writing with me, Sara thought. Why?

For a moment she was tempted to press the issue— just a little. But she held back. There was a fine line between natural curiosity and unhealthy suspicion, and she was afraid of crossing over it.

"What did the lieutenant say?" she asked after a moment's hesitation.

"He's agreed to accept the money for Barbara's medical bills as an interest-free loan. He also said to tell you you're one of the least convincing liars he's ever—ah— attempted to interrogate."

"There go my ambitions for a life of crime," she joked.

"Leave the life of crime to me, Sara," he advised. "As Tank Petrie said the other day, I make a living telling lies."

Sara gave a little laugh, twisting a lock of hair around one finger. "After that remark I think I'm definitely going to have to read your books."

"At the risk of doing myself out of my royalties, let me give you a copy of my last one. I'll even autograph it and underline the good parts."

"I'd rather have you underline the juicy ones," she returned with flirtatious impudence.

"I thought we might read those passages together. In bed."

"That sounds . . . educational."

"You should be warned that I move my lips a lot when I read," he said. "I also have trouble keeping my place . . . so I follow along with my fingers." His voice was velvety with double meaning. Sara shifted in her leather-upholstered swivel chair, her lower body going liquid with yearning.

"Matt—" She swallowed. "I think the Federal Communications Commission or somebody has rules about carrying on this kind of conversation over the telephone."

He laughed. "Why, Sara Lynn Edwards, just what is that mind of yours reading into this perfectly innocent discussion of my literary accomplishments?"

She shifted again. "I—um—I really have to be getting back to work," she told him, taking the coward's way out.

He mocked her retreat with a teasing string of *tsk-tsks*.

"Okay, sweetheart," he said. "Actually, the real reason I called was to ask you to have dinner with me tonight."

"I've had dinner with you every night for the past two weeks."

"I have something a little more meaningful in mind than Chinese take-out."

"I can't think of anything more meaningful than moo shu pork—unless it's your Sicilian spaghetti sauce," she countered.

"Sara—"

"Are you asking me for a date?"

"I've got reservations for two for dinner at seven. If you turn me down, I'll have to take Dingbat, and he doesn't have a thing to wear."

The image of Dingbat shambling into some posh restaurant in all his hairy enormity flitted hilariously through Sara's mind. She fought down a giggle.

"I don't kiss on the first date," she informed him primly.

"Neither does Ding. Neither do I, for that matter. But I'm sure we'll think of *something* to do."

"I might consider doing 'something' on the first date."

"I'll meet you at your office a bit after five and we can discuss it."

"We may never get to dinner."

"I'll chance it. See you in a couple of hours, love."

Sara's bantering conversation with Matt, to say nothing of his parting endearment, left her with a quiet glow. She zipped through the rest of her work with renewed energy, enjoying the professional challenge even as she savored a very personal sense of anticipation.

Although Sara's after-work lifestyle was generally very sedate, she did keep a few items in her desk to boost her daytime look into something appropriate for an evening's socializing. At a few minutes before five she adjourned to the ladies' room to touch up her makeup and redo her hair.

She accented her hazel eyes with a smudge of jade kohl pencil, added an extra coat of black mascara, brushed some coral blush on her cheeks, and refreshed her lip gloss. She then wooshed on a light spray of flowery perfume. Surveying her reflection, she judiciously undid three of the silk-covered buttons at the top of her simply styled dress and retied the sash belt. Finally, she slipped on a pair of gold knot earrings and a matching bracelet.

Ten minutes after she returned to her office, the phone rang.

"Ms. Edwards? He's here!" Doris the receptionist announced without preamble. Her voice held the same breathless excitement it had the first day Matt had shown up at the office. "Mr. M-Michaels is here."

"Thank you, Doris. I'll be right out."

"I'll tell him."

Slightly overweight and with little or no sense of personal style, Doris Cartwright was not a particularly attractive woman. Still, she looked flushed and almost pretty when Sara came into the reception area. Matt was standing by her desk, smiling down at her with easy friendliness. Doris was clutching several ribbon-tied books to her bosom and beaming back at him in undisguised admiration.

He *was* devastatingly good looking in his pale gray linen suit, white silk shirt, and blue patterned silk tie. His highly polished black shoes as well as his narrow belt bore the discreet double-initial Gucci insignia. He radiated expensive assurance and virile elegance.

But his attraction went far beyond that. Sara felt her heartbeat speed up as he turned his attention away from the enraptured Doris and focused on her. His freebooter's grin flashed to life with new intimacy and his laserlike cobalt eyes caressed her with a heat that made her knees go weak.

I'm remembering, are you? his eyes seemed to ask as they went over her.

Oh, yes!

"Are you all set?"

Sara nodded, not quite trusting her voice.

"Wonderful." He took her arm, the touch of his fingers warm and strong through the fine fabric of her sleeve. "Let's go then. Thank you for your help, Doris."

"Oh, thank *you*, Mr. Mathis—I mean, Mr. Michaels! I'll treasure your books forever. Good night, Ms. Edwards."

"Good night, Doris."

Matt guided Sara out to the elevators in the hall. After thumbing the Down button, he pulled her into his arms. "I really did miss you, sweetheart," he told her.

"Mmm—me, too," she breathed.

"God, I like the feel of you in silk." His hands stroked lightly down her back, coming to rest at the curve of her slender waist. "I like the feel of you, period."

"Me, too." There was a provocative curve in the smile she gave him.

"Since our first date hasn't officially started yet, I'm going to kiss you," he announced softly.

It was a liquid, lingering kiss, a teasing, arousing,

caress of mutual pleasuring. Sara flirted her tongue against the tip of his. He responded, deepening the intensity of the kiss for a heady moment before lifting his head.

"Just when does our first date officially start?" she inquired, her gray-green eyes sparkling.

"Maybe never. What do you do on the second date?"

"That depends."

"On what?"

"The first date."

Laughing, he dropped a quick kiss on the tip of her nose.

"You know," he commented, "if this were a Mike Mathis novel, the elevator doors would glide open in a second, I'd swing you up into my arms, carry you inside . . . and we'd make passionate love to each other all the way down to the lobby."

Sara tilted her chin slightly. "Oh?"

As if on cue, a chime sounded, announcing the arrival of the elevator. With a sudden devilish grin Matt swept her off her feet and into his arms. She parted her lips to protest as the elevator doors hissed open. The words died in her throat as she found herself staring into the surprised face of a very respectable-looking middle-aged businessman.

Sara groaned.

"Newlyweds?" the man asked curiously as Matt carried her onto the car with admirable—although, from Sara's point of view, infuriating—aplomb.

"Sprained ankle," she said.

"Elevator phobia," Matt explained.

They spoke simultaneously.

"I beg your pardon?" The elevator door whispered shut.

"I'm terrified of—"

"She tripped over a—"

Their voices clashed again. Sara felt her cheeks go hot. Uncertain of whether she wanted to die of mortification, kill Matt, or simply burst out laughing, she instinctively buried her face against Matt's shoulder. She felt a tremor of reaction run through him.

"She sprained her ankle *and* she's frightened of elevators," Matt said, his voice just a shade too controlled.

"Well," the man said philosophically, "it's really none of my business in any case. Would you like me to press the lobby button for you?"

"Yes, thank you," Matt answered. "As you can see, I've got my hands full at the moment."

A strange sound, somewhere between a snort of indignation and a strangled giggle, came bubbling out of Sara's throat.

"Is she all right?" The man sounded vaguely alarmed.

Oh, lord, she thought, he's probably afraid I'm going to go into hysterics.

She felt another shudder run through Matt's lean body, and realized that he was trying not to laugh.

"There, there, darling," he soothed her in a syrupy tone. "It's the combination of pain and fear," he explained to the other passenger. "She'll be all right once we hit the ground."

I may just hit him, she thought wrathfully. How dare he think this is funny!

The elevator chime sounded again and the car came to a stop. The doors whispered open.

"Ah, well, this is my floor," the man announced politely. "Good—ah—luck."

A few seconds later the elevator resumed its descent.

"Mrrr eee rilly gmmm?" she asked, her face still pressed against Matt's shoulder. She could hear the beating of his heart, smell his distinctive scent.

"Is that a question or are you trying to eat my lapel?" Matt threaded the fingers of one hand through her curly hair and tugged gently, forcing her to lift her head.

"Is he really gone?" she hissed.

"Umm-hmm." He grinned at her.

"Are you going to put me down?" she asked, enunciating each word with icy precision.

She felt him shrug. "Eventually."

"Matt—"

"First, we're going to make passionate love—"

As he started to dip his head, the elevator came to a stop and the doors opened again. This time Sara found herself staring at an extremely well-dressed matron with an equally well-dressed but sullen-faced little boy. Matt swore under his breath. Despite herself, Sara let out a helpless gurgle of laughter and turned her face against his chest once more.

If this were a Mike Mathis novel . . .

She definitely was going to have to read some of Matt's books.

"Are you kidnapping that lady, huh, mister?" the little boy inquired in a piercing voice as the elevator continued its downward journey.

"Martin," the woman reproved.

"How come she's making those weird noises, Mommie? Huh? How come? Is she strangling?"

"Martin!"

"Is she gonna die right here in the elevator?" The child sounded thrilled at the prospect.

Sara was laughing so hard, she was shaking. Matt tightened his grip on her.

"No, Martin," he said. "She's not going to die. But she might get dropped on the floor any second."

"Really, sir—" The woman sniffed. "Martin, get *away*—"

"Can I watch?" Martin demanded, ignoring his mother's expostulations. "D'ya think she'll bounce? I dropped my stupid sister's dumb doll out of the window once, and it bounced."

Sara was having trouble breathing.

The elevator chime sounded once more and the doors slid open.

"This is the lobby, Martin. We're getting out here."

"Un-hunh. He's gonna drop her."

"Martin—"

"I wanna watch! No!"

"Come with Mommie!"

"Nooo-o-o-o!"

"Right this instant! These aren't nice people, Martin!"

Sara shifted herself enough to see the now howling Martin dragged off across the marble expanse of the lobby. She then looked at Matt. He was struggling to keep a straight face. Their eyes met.

"She's right, you know," she informed him solemnly, fingering the smooth surface of his tie. "We *aren't* nice people."

"Speak for yourself, sweetheart," he retorted, carrying her off the elevator. "Unless, of course, you want to find out if you bounce."

"You wouldn't dare!" she gasped.

Breaking into a grin, he put her gently back on her feet. They stared at each other for a long moment, then began laughing. Several people brushed by them, giving them sharp, curious looks.

"E-elevator pho-phobia?" Sara finally managed to sputter out. "Where did you get that?"

He took a steadying breath and ran his hand through his neatly brushed black hair. "I'm a writer, remember? It was a hell of a lot more original than your sprained-ankle routine, I must say." He leaned against the wall, chuckling. "I think I'll put Martin in one of my books."

"I didn't realize you wrote juvenile horror stories."

"I'll have someone kidnap him."

"And his parents refuse to pay to get him back, right? I think O. Henry already used that plot in 'The Ransom of Red Chief.'"

"You're a CPA, Sara, not a literary critic," he declared with mock disdain.

"Speaking of literary critics—" She swallowed, about

to broach a subject that had been nagging at her. "Doris Cartwright knew who you were that first day, didn't she? *That's* why she was so excited."

He hesitated for a moment, then cocked a dark brow in sardonic emphasis. "I have the same effect on women who don't know who I am," he commented. "Look at how you reacted to me in the beginning."

"Matt—"

He grimaced, straightening up. "Okay, yes. Your receptionist did know who I was. She's a fan and she apparently recognized me from some talk show I was on."

"She didn't say anything."

"I asked her not to. I told her I was—ah—undercover, so to speak. Incognito."

"And she just accepted that?"

"Are you joking? She did everything but swear herself to secrecy with a blood oath."

"Doris Cartwright?" Sara looked and sounded skeptical.

"Sara, she wasn't excited about me. She was excited about Mike Mathis."

"But you are—does Mike Mathis make a practice of going around asking strange women to keep his identity a mystery?"

"If you believe the gossip, that's the least of what he asks them to do." There was an odd tension in his voice and she saw something almost challenging flicker through the depths of his blue eyes.

"Oh." Catching her breath, she bit her lip and dropped her lashes.

"Sara..." His tone softened. He put a finger under her chin and raised it with gentle force.

She met his gaze and sighed, hating the feelings roiling up within her. "I—I'm sorry," she said finally.

He shook his head. "Don't be sorry. We both know this is going to take some time. Trusting always does.

But I promise you, Sara, I'm not Mike Mathis—not with you."

But I don't know who Mike Mathis is, she protested silently. And I barely know Mathieson Michaels!

She moistened her lips delicately and summoned up a smile. "Well, whoever you are—do you still want to take me to dinner?"

He ran his finger lightly down the smooth line of her throat and into the soft V of skin revealed by her discreetly unbuttoned bodice. "I want to take you to a lot of places," he told her. "Dinner will do for a start."

They had dinner at the Cafe des Artistes, a well-known restaurant on Manhattan's Upper West Side. It was an unabashedly romantic place that captured the stylish elegance of the 1930s. The mirrored barroom where they lingered over pre-dinner drinks was a perfect setting for witty repartee and flirtatious dalliance, and the artfully lighted dining area—decorated by a delightful collection of peach-toned nudes by muralist Howard Chandler Christy—seemed designed for a lovers' rendezvous.

On Matt's recommendation, Sara began with gravlax. The restaurant's version of the famous Scandinavian dish was delicious. The raw salmon had been marinated in salt, pepper, sugar, and dill and was served in shimmering red-pink slices with a dusting of freshly ground pepper and a zesty mustard sauce.

For their entrees Matt ordered lamb chops with Béarnaise and Sara, feeling especially hungry, chose roast duckling. The bird was moist and meltingly tender, with deliciously crisp skin. Instead of the usual accompaniment of orange or cherry sauce, it came dressed with a delicately flavored mixture of apples and Calvados. They traded bites of food and morsels of intimate conversation with innocent, unshadowed enjoyment.

"Dessert," Matt said with relish, flipping open the menu as the waiter cleared away the dishes from their main course.

"Mmm—" Sara sipped at her glass of rosé wine, eyeing the list of delectable temptations. "I really shouldn't."

"We can work it off later," he promised blandly, his blue eyes gleaming as he glanced across the table at her.

"Do you have any idea how many calories there are in chocolate mousse cake? Or frozen mocha and praline cake?"

"We can work *very* hard."

"What's the Great Dessert Plate?"

"Samples of just about everything on the dessert menu piled onto one great plate."

She sighed. "And the special chocolate torte?"

"I've never had it, but I've been told it's what they feed chocaholics when they die and go to heaven."

Sara laughed. "Fortunately, chocolate isn't one of my vices."

"Would you care to tell me what is?"

"You're the writer," she countered with a sparkle. "Use your imagination."

"Sweetheart, I've already used my imagination for two full weeks where you're concerned. That part of me's tired."

"What about the rest of you?"

He closed the menu with a slow, sexy grin. "How does the idea of having dessert back at the apartment sound?"

"Have you decided what you'd like?" the waiter asked pleasantly, hovering by Matt's elbow, his pencil poised.

Matt lifted one brow as if to signify he'd decided what he wanted, but it wasn't on the menu. Sara lowered her lashes and cleared her throat.

"I think I'd like the fresh strawberries, please," she said softly.

"Coffee?"

"I'd prefer tea."

"Sir?"

"Just coffee, thank you."

"No dessert?" Sara inquired after the waiter moved away.

"I can wait."

"You may have to roll me home after this meal."

"As long as I don't have to carry you onto any elevators."

"Do you think I would have bounced if you'd dropped me?"

"Like Martin's stupid sister's dumb doll?"

They both laughed.

"Do the heroes of your books really sweep women off their feet and into elevators to make passionate love all the way down to the lobby?" she asked after a minute.

Matt finished the last of his wine. A lock of his dark hair had curved down onto his forehead, and Sara's fingers itched to push it back into place.

"Actually, only one of my heroes ever did it, and I think the elevator was on the way up."

"Maybe that's what went wrong with us today," she observed thoughtfully as the waiter returned. He served the coffee and tea and placed cream, sugar, and lemon on the table. He then presented Sara with a large dish of jewel-red strawberries topped with a cloud-white drift of whipped cream. After a brief check to ensure that all their needs were satisfied, he departed. "After all," she continued, picking up her spoon, "I don't imagine your characters conduct their love scenes in front of an audience."

"No," he conceded with a quick grin. "If we *had* been in a Mike Mathis novel back at your office, the elevator would have been empty. It also would have gotten stuck between floors for at least an hour."

Sara sampled her berries. The fruit was fresh and sweet and ripe with juice. "I'm afraid reality never quite lives up to fiction."

He drank some of his coffee, studying her with caressing intensity. "That depends on the reality, sweetheart. Nothing I got down on paper today came close to matching what I experienced with you last night . . . and this morning."

Sara licked a dab of cream off her lips. "Did you—did you write today?" she asked a bit breathlessly.

He nodded, his expression becoming oddly abstracted for a moment. "Yes."

She spooned up another mouthful of strawberries. "I've never known a writer before," she commented after a moment. "I wonder—how do you work? So many hours a day? So many words?"

"It depends. Once I'm done with the research and the basic outline, I tend to become somewhat obsessed with getting the story down on paper. It isn't a regularized, disciplined thing."

"Do you tell people what you're writing beforehand?"

"Not anymore than I can help. Lydia is always accusing me of being too secretive about my work." He shrugged. "Someone once said something to the effect that a work of literature, like a baby in the womb, shouldn't be brought out before it's fully developed. I suppose that's my philosophy."

Sara added a squeeze of fresh lemon to her tea and then stirred in a spoonful of sugar. "Do you use a typewriter or a word processor?" she asked curiously. She didn't recall seeing either of those items in the baggage he had brought into the apartment.

"Neither. The basic reason for that is that my typing skills are virtually nil. I'm a practitioner of the Columbus method."

"What's the Columbus method?"

He grinned boyishly. "Discover a key and land on it."

She smiled. "What do you do then? Dictate your work?"

He shook his head. "I've always written out everything in longhand. And when my first handwritten novel turned out to be successful, I decided I shouldn't mess with a winning formula. Once I get my first draft done, I send a photocopy of it to a typing service here in the city. I work with their typed version when it comes to making revisions."

"Do you have to revise a lot?"

"Sometimes. It's usually fine tuning, not major surgery. My writing tends to come out of my head in pretty much its final form, first draft."

"Does the typist have trouble with your handwriting?"

"My handwriting is very legible, but I'm reliably informed that my spelling is atrocious."

"You can't spell and you haven't reconciled your checkbook in two years. I'm shocked." She pulled a teasing look of reproach.

"You're supposed to be shocked at the things I can do and have done, Sara."

"Are you talking about last night?"

"Mmm . . . or this morning."

"Well, I do admit I was a little *surprised* that a man who can't balance his accounts can balance so many other things—and in a shower, no less!"

"I confess I have developed a certain interest in— ah—the bottom line since I met you."

They finished their meal a short time later and left the restaurant hand in hand.

"Do you want to walk?" Matt asked.

"Back to the apartment?"

"No, just walk."

"All right."

They strolled leisurely down Broadway, pausing for a few moments across from Lincoln Center. Sara raised her eyes admiringly to the great stone and glass front of the Metropolitan Opera House. The building was brilliantly lit against the night darkness, with its two famed Marc Chagall murals in the upper windows in inspiring testament to the whimsy of an artistic genius.

"Are we going anywhere in particular?" she wondered aloud as they continued their ramble. It was a beautifully clear night, full of possibilities and promises.

"The Plaza hotel," he told her, heading them east.

"The Plaza?"

"More or less."

"What does that mean?"

What it actually meant was the Central Park South corner *across* from the hotel.

"A hansom cab ride!" Sara exclaimed delightedly as she realized his intention.

"I did say I thought we should save this sort of thing for a beautiful moonlit night," he reminded her. He glanced upward. "It seems to me tonight fits the bill perfectly."

"Yes," she agreed, her smile very sweet.

He bowed and gestured toward the line of horsedrawn cabs. "In that case, madam, your carriage awaits."

Chapter 8

"WHIPPED CREAM?" SARA wondered aloud, turning the page with a breathy little laugh.

It was Friday night and she was sitting in bed reading, her book propped on her sheet-covered knees. The bedside lamp was the only light on in the room and it bathed her with a soft, extremely flattering glow. Her casually brushed hair gleamed in a fiery halo of curls and her fair skin had a warm, inviting sheen. The narrow strap of her simple cream-colored satin nightgown had slipped off her right shoulder. She shrugged it back into place in an unthinking movement.

Her eyes widened slightly as she came to a particularly erotic passage. In the middle of reading it she glanced toward the bathroom door. She had heard the shower shut off a few moments before. A small, delicious smile of feminine anticipation played across her lips.

She and Matt were now "living together" in every sense of the phrase. Although he continued to use the spare room for storage and work space, he'd moved himself and many of his personal items into the master bedroom. Aside from a few minor points of friction— her tendency to hog all the sheets, his fondness for singing amazingly raunchy ditties from his army days in the shower—the arrangement was wonderfully satisfying for both of them.

To fall asleep in Matt's arms at night and to wake up next to him in the morning gave Sara a sense of security and happiness she had never experienced, had never really dared hope to experience.

She moistened her lips, rereading a paragraph with a soft little sigh before she flipped the page. She looked toward the bathroom door again.

True to his promise, Matt had given her an autographed copy of his most recent book. She had also picked up his previous novels in paperback at a bookstore near her office. She'd quickly learned why he was a bestselling author, and why readers, especially *women* readers, fantasized about the kind of man Mike Mathis must be.

She was particularly fascinated by the way his writing skills developed from book to book . . . and by the way he obviously drew on his personal experiences in his work. His most recent book, *Tin Pigeon*, was about a veteran police officer caught in the middle of a political squeeze play. Sara saw a great deal of Tank Petrie in one of the secondary characters, and she had a sense that Lieutenant Joseph Santini had served as a model for the protagonist. She was impressed by the elegant economy of Matt's language and intrigued, but made a bit uneasy, by his insights into people's personal dreams and private disgraces.

The door to the bathroom swung open and Matt strolled out, a towel wrapped about his hips. Sara set the book down in her lap. His black hair was slightly damp and brushed straight back off his forehead, emphasizing the hawkish strength of his features.

Sara's eyes skimmed his body with a mixture of provocativeness and possession as she admired his lean, muscled symmetry. Matt did not make a fetish of fitness the way some men Sara knew did, but he took a frank and very easy pleasure in his physicality. He also made no secret of the fact that he thoroughly enjoyed Sara's conditioned slenderness and athleticism. Having become used to running a poor second to Chrissie's statuesque ripeness, Sara was surprised and unabashedly delighted by his open appreciation.

"What are you reading? Must be *some* book." He grinned, stretching once, then flexed his shoulders.

"Why do you say that?"

"Well, modesty prevents me from suggesting that I'm the one who's put that lustful expression in those gorgeous hazel eyes of yours."

"I didn't know modesty ever prevented you from doing anything."

"Ouch."

"Anyway, my expression isn't lustful, it's—ah—wait a second—" She quickly riffled back through the pages of the book in her lap. "Here it is. My expression is 'full of promises a lady never makes but always keeps.'"

"I like the sound of that."

"I should hope so!" She stuck a bookmark between the pages, closed the volume, and held it up. "See?"

The vivid crimson, black, and white cover of the paperback had an eye-catching graphic simplicity. The boldly lettered title said *Running Scared*. Beneath that was the declaration: A NOVEL BY MIKE MATHIS.

Matt looked surprised. "I do have a way with words, don't I?"

"Ummm . . . you have a way with a lot of things." She put the book on the bedside table beside the lamp as he sat down on the edge of the mattress.

"Would you care to elaborate on that?" The strap of her nightgown had slipped again and he reached forward to tug it back into place. His fingers lingered on the soft curve of her upper arm for several delicious seconds, sending tiny frissons of pleasurable awareness dancing along her nerve ends.

"Modesty prevents me," she said, using his previous phrase.

"Funny how it didn't prevent you from assaulting me in the living room the other night when you got home from work. The shades were up and it was still light out. There's no telling who witnessed that depraved little episode."

"You should have considered that before you draped yourself over the couch wearing nothing but a 'welcome home' sign."

"How was I to know you'd misinterpret a friendly little greeting? Besides, the reason I didn't have anything on was that it was ninety-five degrees outside and I was hot."

"You certainly were." She traced a line up his hair-rough chest, fluttering her lashes demurely. "At least you're nice and cool now."

"Don't count on it."

Cupping the back of her head in the palm of one hand, he pulled her face to his for a slow, expert kiss. She returned the caress with eagerness, bringing her arms up around his neck. He nipped teasingly at her lower lip, then traced the curving line of it with the tip of his tongue. Afterward he feathered a trail of kisses down her throat and nuzzled erotically at the warm, sweetly scented hollow of her collarbone.

"Mmm—Matt?" She tilted her head back languidly, her fingers stroking over his shoulders.

"What?" He was nibbling at her flesh with drugging delicacy.

"Doesn't—ah—the whipped cream get on the sheets?"

His mouth sought and saluted the shadowed cleft between her breasts. "Hmmm?"

"It must be a little m-messy." She caught her breath as his lips closed over one of her nipples, sucking at the hardening tip through the fabric of her nightgown. She gasped when she felt the brief but gentle bite of his teeth.

He lifted his head after a moment, amusement and arousal plain in his gemstone eyes. "What are you talking about?"

"In your book. When the hero goes to bed with the call girl to get the information he needs, she uses whipped cream—"

"And?"

"And, I was wondering, well, it sounded gooey."

"But very good."

"I suppose."

"To tell the truth, it gets messy only if you use chocolate sauce."

"Choc—are you talking about sex or making sundaes?"

"I hear there's something to be said for strawberry jam, too."

"Matt!"

"Of course, that really ruins the sheets."

"Have you ever—" A very ribald pun flitted through Sara's mind, bringing an unexpected blush to her cheeks. Matt grinned diabolically, obviously reading her thought.

"Naughty, naughty," he reproved playfully.

"No," she returned hoarsely, a wanton sparkle coming into her eyes as she reached for the towel at his waist. *"This* is naughty."

"So, Matty tells me you had me figured for an enforcer," Tank Petrie growled at Sara about a week later. They were sitting across from each other in a small, out-of-the-way restaurant on Manhattan's Lower East Side.

Matt had gone up to the bar to get Tank and himself another round of beers.

The get-together had been a spur-of-the-moment thing. Tank had called the apartment asking for Matt, apparently wanting to check on the situation with Lieutenant Santini. He'd ended up proposing a quick dinner for the three of them. Sara, whose curiosity about Mathieson Michaels—and Mike Mathis—was still far from satisfied, had willingly gone along with the idea.

"Enforcer?" she repeated uncertainly. Tank had spent much of the meal regaling her with stories of Matt's adventures during his period as an "observer" with the police department.

"Yeah. You know—hired muscle. A bonebreaker."

"Oh." She grimaced, dipping a french fry into the puddle of ketchup on her deluxe hamburger platter. "I apologize for what I thought. It's just that there were a lot of unexplained things about Matt back then, and the two of you were very cryptic the day we met in the subway. Matt told me—later—about your being a police officer. I am sorry."

Petrie scratched his crooked nose. "Hey, I understand. With this ugly mug of mine, I'm surprised you didn't think worse." The big man started to chuckle as Matt returned to the booth, placing two moisture-hazed glasses of beer on the table before he slid in next to Sara. "Of course, I can see why you'd have your suspicions about old Blue Eyes here."

Matt put an arm around Sara's shoulders. "You're still mad because I didn't fall for the alligator-in-the-sewer scam you run on all the rookies."

"Nah." Tank took a deep swallow of his beer. "I never figured you would. A writer type like you, I knew you'd spot the con a mile off. But I *am* kinda irked you put that stuff about the police groupies in *Tin Pigeon*. Ever since my wife read it, she's convinced I'm cheating on her with some sweet young thing who's got the hots for the guys in blue, just like in your book."

"Did you remind her you're plainclothes, not uniform?"

"Right. A big bunch of good *that's* going to do." Tank gulped down some beer with a disgruntled slurp. "I spend eight hours sweating in an unmarked car, bored out of my skull, keeping some scummy drug dealer under surveillance, and when I come home my wife starts checking my collar for lipstick stains!"

"How long have you been married, Tank?" Sara asked, sensing that this grousing was more for effect than for anything else.

"Eighteen years come December." His expression softened.

"Do you have any children?"

"Yeah, two. One of each. Here, let me show you." He pulled a battered wallet out of his back pants pocket and flipped it open with undisguised pride. "This is my wife, Alice. I call her Tiny," he declared gruffly.

Sara had to smile. The woman in the photograph looked about five seven and was very generously proportioned. On the other hand, compared with Tank she did have a certain air of fragility.

"She's very attractive," Sara said sincerely.

"These are my kids. That's Joey. He's sixteen and plays football in school. This is Jennie. She's going on fifteen and wants to be a lawyer. Can you beat that? She's also got a heavy-duty crush on Matty, but I figure she'll grow out of it."

Matt took a sip of beer. "Jennie hasn't seen me in more than a year, Tank," he replied mildly, unruffled by the friendly needling.

"Yeah, well, you made a big impression on her. She thinks you're hotter stuff than that hairy rock singer she's always listening to." Tank drained his glass. "You know, you're not bad with kids," he observed offhandedly. "Ever think about settling down and having a few of your own?"

The question triggered a strange surge of emotion within Sara. She deliberately avoided looking at Matt.

"By myself?" he countered wryly, making a joke out of it.

Tank snorted, crumpling his paper napkin and dropping it on the table. "Ha-ha. It was just a passing thought. Who knows, though. If you got married and started a family, you might get some good material for another one of your best sellers."

"Tank." The humor had gone out of Matt's voice. Sara felt the sudden tension in his body.

"Okay, okay." The other man made a palms-up gesture. "Subject closed. A smart guy like you, who drops out of Yale to join the army, who hangs out with cops and crooks when he ought to be hobnobbing with the jet set, who more or less works for a living when he could be sponging off his seven-figure trust fund, doesn't need suggestions from *me* about how to live his life. No way."

Matt shook his head. "When you put it like that, it sounds as though what I need is psychiatric help."

"You said it, I didn't," Tank returned with a brief grin. His slate-gray eyes moved in Sara's direction. She managed to summon up a casual smile. "Could be something else you need, too. But, like I said, the subject's closed. Now, you want another beer? I'll buy this time."

"I'm sorry if Tank made you uncomfortable," Matt said during the cab ride back to the apartment.

Sara shook her head. "It's all right."

"He has a habit of sticking his nose into things."

"Maybe that's why he became a policeman."

"Maybe." He smiled for a moment. The expression didn't reach his eyes. They remained pensive, almost withdrawn.

"He likes you, Matt."

"Mmm." It was neither a yes nor a no. He shifted in the seat and looked at her steadily for several seconds.

"Do you ever think about settling down? About having children? Or did your father and Gary sour you on that?"

She couldn't get a fix on his tone or on the reason for his unexpected questions.

"I—of course, I think about it," she said slowly, picking her words with care. "But I'm not pursuing the idea of marriage the way I'm, say, pursuing my career. If I find someone, or he finds me . . ." She chewed her lower lip, trying to articulate her feelings. "I don't like to think I've been soured, but I am more . . . wary."

"Trust equals love equals getting hurt."

"I hope not," she said with soft sincerity, her face taking on a vulnerable look. She closed her eyes with a sigh as Matt gathered her against him and took her mouth in a hot, hungry kiss.

August was an enchanted month. The parts of Sara's soul that had been chilled—blighted, really—by her father's faithlessness and Gary's betrayal warmed and blossomed. She was at her best with Matt as they laughed and loved together, sometimes with aching tenderness, sometimes with overwhelming passion.

Deep inside she knew the heated, halcyon days of summer would not last forever, but it was a knowledge she tried to keep at bay. Matt didn't speak about the future—not his, not hers, not theirs. So neither did she.

"I think I'm considering having an affair," Elayne Berman announced to Sara as she scraped the remains of dinner into the garbage disposal. "How would you feel about sharing Matt?"

Sara smiled, wrapping some leftovers in foil and putting them into the refrigerator. "How would Paul feel about sharing you?"

"Spoilsport," her friend retorted. "He *is* gorgeous, you know."

"Who? Paul?"

"No. Matt! And don't give me that innocent but-I-love-him-for-his-mind stare, Sara Edwards." Elayne wrinkled her nose thoughtfully. "It is love, isn't it?" she asked seriously.

Sara sighed. Characteristically, Elayne had ferreted out the details of her changed relationship with Matt. Equally characteristically, she had decided she wanted to meet Matt for herself. A dinner at the Bermans' loft in SoHo had eventually been arranged. So far the evening had been a rousing success.

"Yes," Sara admitted. "I'm in love with him."

"And he's in love with you."

Sara smiled with a trace of wistfulness. There had been no further declarations since the first night they had made love.

"Well, you deserve, kiddo," Elayne declared, beginning to load the dishwasher. "I suppose you've been trying to find a place to live? What's-his-name is coming back to reclaim his apartment pretty soon, isn't he?"

"His name is Lowell. His lawyer has renewed his lease on the apartment, but he's decided to extend his stay in Switzerland for a few more months. Matt and I are still subletting. That is, Matt is subletting from Lowell and I'm sub-subletting from him."

"Ah, the wonders of New York leasing arrangements." Elayne gestured expansively with a pair of cooking utensils. "But you still haven't answered my question."

"Things are . . . a bit up in the air, Elayne."

"Oh-ho. And until they come down, you'd just as soon I minded my own business?"

"Well—"

"Say no more. He is crazy about you, though." She giggled suddenly, her brown eyes fizzy with amusement. "And to think you once thought he might be a criminal or something."

"Don't remind me." A slightly edited version of the entire misunderstanding about Matt had come out over dinner.

"If only you'd mentioned *Mathieson* Michaels that day at the health club, I would have been able to set you straight. Paul is a big fan of his, even though Mike Mathis is making a fortune for another publishing house."

"I felt like an idiot when I found out the truth."

"Why? It seems to me you had some very valid reasons for thinking what you did. Of course, your very valid reasons were totally *wrong*."

"Thanks, Elayne."

"You're welcome. Is Matt going to dedicate his next book to you?"

"I think that depends on the book," Sara replied lightly.

"So, can you at least give me a hint?"

"About his next book? He hasn't even given me one."

"Oh." Elayne rearranged several glasses before shutting the dishwasher. "You know, I've always had this fantasy about having some great work of literature dedicated to me," she revealed. "I suppose that's one of the reasons I was so attracted to Paul in the beginning. I figured as an editor at a publishing house he could introduce me to somebody . . . ." She smiled and shrugged. "I just think it would be terribly romantic."

A mischievous light sparkled in Sara's gray-green eyes. "Matt dedicated his first novel to a man named Elmo, who was his physical therapist. He says Elmo inspired the revenge fantasies that led him to start writing."

"Yuck," Elayne commented with a grimace, taking a moment to digest this revelation. "Well, maybe you should forget about the dedication then and settle for a copy of his next book signed 'Love, Matt.'"

"I don't think it was such a good idea to have told Paul and Elayne about my thinking you were Lydia Follett's . . . you know," Sara murmured drowsily several hours later. She and Matt had made slow, sweet love after returning home from the Bermans', deliberately prolonging each touch, savoring each exquisite sensation, never hurrying toward the ultimate pleasure they knew they would eventually achieve.

"They seemed to find it very funny," he observed, teasing her tousled hair with his fingers. She was curled up against him, her head resting in the taut curve of his shoulder. She watched the steady rise and fall of his naked chest.

"But, still—"

"In any case, I took your thinking that I was Lydia's 'you know' as a compliment."

"A *compliment?*" she echoed skeptically, stroking his torso with one palm. Beneath the sheets their legs remained in an intimately familiar tangle. She could feel the stirrings of his response to her touch. "I thought you'd be insulted."

"That shows how much you know, sweetheart."

The comment sent a strange pang lancing through her. She shivered a little.

"Sara?" Matt lifted his head to look at her, his blue eyes sharp.

"Nothing," she said quickly. "I suppose—well, you did laugh a lot when I told you."

"I have an odd sense of humor. I do admit I was a little taken aback to learn that a CPA of your skill had been adding two and two and coming up with five where I was concerned, but, frankly, I was flattered you thought I could make a decent living as a professional sex object."

"A *decent* living wasn't what I thought you were making."

Matt shifted, levering himself up on one elbow so he could gaze down at her. "I think I'm going to leave that line alone," he remarked with a grin.

"Too bad. I was hoping you'd follow it to its logical conclusion."

"Get down to the bottom line again, hmm?"

"Not exact—ah! *Matt!*" She arched abruptly as his free hand sought out one of the most sensitive parts of her body. A star shower of pleasure radiated out from her core. She gave a shuddery sigh when he caressed her again, his expression very intent as he watched her reaction.

"There's no conclusion—logical or otherwise—for us," he told her huskily. "Trust me, Sara." He kissed her, his mouth feathering over hers provocatively.

He took her lips before she could tell him that more than anything else in the world she wanted to believe she could.

Chapter 9

CHRISSIE SHOWED UP totally without warning on the Saturday before Labor Day.

Sara was in the midst of mixing the batter for a devil's food cake when she heard someone knocking at the apartment door. She and Matt had decided to drive to Connecticut for a country holiday weekend at an inn Elayne and Paul Berman had recommended. They planned to stop for a picnic on the way, and the cake was her contribution to the menu. Matt had gone out to shop for the rest of the food and to take care of a long list of errands, including kenneling Dingbat for the weekend and getting himself a long overdue haircut.

"Just a minute!" she called, wiping her hands on her jeans. She headed for the door, wondering who in the world it could be.

"Sara? Open up! It's me!"

Sara closed her eyes for a moment. She didn't have to look through the peephole to identify who "me" was.

She took a deep breath and squared her shoulders.

"Hold on, Chrissie," she said after a moment, unlocking the door. She swung it open, mentally bracing herself for almost anything.

"Ta-da!" Chrissie trilled gaily, striking an old-fashioned glamour-girl pose with one hand on her hip and the other behind her head. "Surprise!" She was wearing a body-hugging black T-shirt dress and strappy sandals. Her red-blond hair billowed around her shoulders in artful disarray. Her lightly tanned face was made up in a "natural look" that probably took a full hour and two dozen different types of cosmetics to achieve.

"Hello, Chrissie," Sara said a trifle warily.

Chrissie dropped the pose. "Hi! Aren't you going to invite me in?"

"Of course. Come in."

Chrissie stepped into the apartment and glanced around with undisguised interest as Sara shut the door.

"He's not here," Sara told her dryly.

"Oh?" Her sister's eyes widened in innocent inquiry. It was one of her best expressions. Sara wondered if she still practiced it in the mirror. "Who?"

"Mathieson Michaels."

"Oh!"

"You remember him, don't you? Lowell's stepbrother? The man who had the legal right to the apartment you sublet to me? The man you warned me was the black sheep of his family? The man you spilled my entire life's story to over the phone?"

Chrissie dismissed that little episode with a casual wave of her hand. "Oh, that! It's all in the past, anyway.

"Why did you tell Matt so much about me?"

"Well, he wanted to know," Chrissie answered with a mixture of impatience and defensiveness. "Besides, it all worked out, didn't it? And by the time I told him about you, I knew who he really was." Her green eyes took on a heightened sparkle. "I nearly freaked when I found out!"

"You're talking about the fact that Matt writes under the name Mike Mathis."

"He *is* Mike Mathis!" Chrissie gave a little shiver. "I think it's so exciting."

"Chrissie—"

"You know, they say he does a lot of—um—*personal* research for his books," her sister observed slyly. "I don't suppose—"

"Look—" Sara suspected Chrissie was being thoughtless rather than deliberately malicious. But it didn't help.

"He was out in L.A. doing a screen treatment earlier this year," Chrissie chattered on. "I really hate Lowell for not saying anything about being related to him. How stuffy and mean can somebody be? Of course, he never liked my acting career very much, so he probably went out of his way not to help me with it. Then again, screenwriters don't have that much pull in the industry. But, still . . . *Mike Mathis*." She savored the name dreamily.

"His name is Matt Michaels," Sara corrected her sister. "And, as I said before, he's not here."

Chrissie frowned, her lushly glossed lips forming a childish pout. "Now, don't be nasty, Sara. I didn't come to see Mike—Matt—whatever. And even if I had, I'm not going to be around long enough to do any harm to whatever you have going with him. You *do* have something going, don't you? Hmmm?"

Sara was left speechless for a moment by the truly remarkable insensitivity of her sister's words. A small part of her felt a twinge of helplessness at Chrissie's bold confidence in her own irresistibility.

"Chrissie, what are you doing here?" she asked finally.

"Well, to tell you the truth, I've got terrific news. I've got a part in a movie!"

"A part in a—" Sara stared, totally caught off balance.

"Umm-hmm." Chrissie turned on a dazzling, self-satisfied smile, clearly encouraging any admiring remarks her sister might want to make.

Sara was still a bit stunned. "That's—wonderful," she said at last. After a moment she cleared her throat and tried for a little more emotion. "Really, I'm very happy for you. This is wonderful news."

Chrissie preened. "It's a featured role," she explained. "I read for the part when I first went out to Hollywood, but they gave it to somebody else." A quick twist of her mouth indicated her opinion of that decision. "I figured that was the end of it. Then I got this frantic call from my agent last night. It seems the other actress had an accident—broke both arms—and the producer wants me to replace her. Isn't that *great?*"

Sara carefully refrained from saying that she sincerely doubted whether the other actress felt that way. "But—but why are you here in New York? Is the movie being filmed in Manhattan?"

Chrissie laughed and tossed her head. "No. It's being shot in Rome. Can you believe it? Me! I'm going to Rome! I'm flying out of Kennedy late this afternoon. The reason I'm here is that I left my passport in Lowell's desk when I went to L.A., and I need it." She suddenly threw her arms around Sara in an enthusiastic hug. "I am so-o-o happy! I know this is the big break I've been waiting for. And, I tell you what—when I get to be rich, you can help manage my money."

"Thank you," Sara said dryly, disengaging herself.

Chrissie glanced at her watch. "Oh, I really have to get a move on. I want to do a little shopping before I take off. I have hardly a thing to wear. Ah—everything is still pretty much the way it was, isn't it? You haven't moved things around, have you?"

"I—no." Sara seldom went into the spare room. "I think Matt's been using Lowell's desk for his writing."

"Oh." Chrissie looked interested. "Well, that's great. Look, you go back to whatever it was you were doing before and I'll dig up my passport. It shouldn't take very long."

"Chrissie." Sara shifted a bit uneasily. "I don't know if you should—I wish you'd wait before you go through the desk. Matt should be home soon, and I'm sure he'd want—"

"—to meet me?" Chrissie finished, completely oblivious to what Sara was trying to say. "I'd love to meet him, too. Believe me, I would. But I don't have much time. Don't worry, I'll be very neat."

With a strange combination of resignation and uncertainty Sara watched silently as her sister brushed blithely by her and headed toward the spare room.

Chrissie Edwards, you are one of a kind, she thought.

A few seconds later she shrugged and went back to the kitchen.

She had the cake in the oven by the time her sister emerged triumphantly from the spare room.

"Did you find what you were looking for?" Sara asked as she set the timer and began to rinse the utensils and bowls she had been using.

"Umm-hmm. But that's not all I found."

Something in Chrissie's tone sent a prickle of apprehension up Sara's spine. She turned. "What are you talking about?"

"This," Chrissie said with dramatic succinctness. She was standing in the kitchen doorway gripping her blue-bound, gold-embossed passport with one hand and brandishing a sheaf of yellow writing paper with the other. Sara's heart leapt into her throat when she realized what her sister was holding. Even from a distance of six or seven feet Matt's bold, angular script was easily recognizable. Sara had been seeing it filling in *The New York Times* crossword puzzle every day for nearly two months.

"What are you doing with that?"

"You could have at least told me Mike Mathis was writing something based on you!" Chrissie said. "It was bad enough that Lowell didn't tell me anything, but you—my own sister! If they make a movie out of this—and they probably will—I'll just bet I'd have the inside track for a big role."

Sara hadn't heard anything beyond the first sentence. It hit her like a bolt of electricity. "Matt isn't writing anything about me," she said, her tone very stark.

"Oh, really?" Chrissie scoffed. "Well, maybe this will refresh your memory." Clearing her throat melodramatically, Chrissie proceeded to read a detailed description of a woman in her late twenties, a woman with stubbornly curly mahogany hair, changeable hazel eyes, and a freckled nose, who was afraid to give herself to love because of past betrayals.

For a moment Sara thought she might be physically ill. Fighting down a wave of nausea, she reached for the papers. "Chrissie—"

Her sister danced back a step or two. "And what about this?" she asked.

"Don't!"

Chrissie started to read again. This time the passage she chose was a love scene—a love scene Sara knew very well. Every endearment, every kiss, every caress was set down in passionate explicitness. The language was unabashedly, evocatively erotic.

Her face pale except for a patch of scarlet on each cheek, Sara snatched the pages away from Chrissie. "That's none of your business!" she said, her voice shaking with outrage. It was none of *anybody's* business! She felt herself going cold and closed up inside.

Oh, God, she thought, all Matt's talk about "literary inspiration" and this—this!—was the result. Sara felt violated and dirty.

Chrissie stared at her, obviously bemused by her violent reaction. "What's the matter with you?" she demanded in an irritated tone.

"You—you shouldn't have gone through Matt's things."

"Oh, for heaven's sake! What are they? Top secret? Mike Mathis is a best-selling author!"

"His name is Matt Michaels!"

"What difference does that make?"

A lot, Sara thought. It makes a lot of difference—all the difference in the world. She had trusted Mathieson Michaels.

"Chrissie—" she began painfully, her voice taut. She wanted her sister to leave. She needed desperately to be alone.

"Didn't you know he was writing about you?"

Reluctantly, Sara shook her head.

"Oh." Chrissie wrinkled her nose. "Well, maybe he didn't want you to get inhibited," she suggested offhandedly. "I mean, if you'd known, maybe you wouldn't have acted like youself. Although I never thought you had it in you to act like *that*." She gestured toward the papers Sara still had clutched in one fist.

Sara gave a strangled laugh. Better that than bursting into tears. "'Smile, you're on *Candid Camera*,'" she intoned with bitter irony.

"Exactly!" Chrissie nodded, visibly pleased to have gotten her point across. "Of course, it's an X-rated *Candid Camera*, but—" She gestured airily, then consulted her watch. "Oops! I really have got to be going. I figure maybe an hour or so in Bloomingdale's and I'll be able to come with a few things to put me in the mood for *la dolce vita*."

"I'm sure you'll do just fine," Sara returned automatically. A strange kind of numbness was stealing over her. She knew she was shattering into a thousand jagged pieces inside, but she couldn't feel the pain. She couldn't feel anything.

"I wish I could meet Mike Mathis, but—" Chrissie shrugged philosophically. "I do expect an autographed copy of his next book." Smiling, she brushed a kiss against Sara's cheek. "Ta-ta, sis. Wish me luck."

Sara's lips curved crookedly. "Good luck, Chrissie."

Sara had no real memory of how she got through the next two hours. Blank-faced, she tidied up around the apartment, took the cake out of the oven, took a shower and changed her clothes, and covered the cake with a rich fudge icing. Although she performed these tasks with her usual efficiency, she took no satisfaction, no sense of accomplishment, from them. She was a fragile, emptied vessel, devoid of all emotion. Deep within her was the dull, throbbing awareness that when she did begin to feel again, she would experience the worst pain she had known in her life.

She was sitting at the kitchen table, her hands folded like a schoolgirl, when Matt finally returned. His manuscript was at the end of the table, neatly stacked, the somewhat crumpled pages smoothed to the best of her shaky-fingered ability.

She hadn't dared read any more of it than Chrissie had read aloud. She'd been tempted to, of course, just as she'd been tempted to rip each and every sheet into tiny shreds. But once she'd put the sheaf of papers down, she'd been unable to bring herself to touch them again.

When, she wondered, had Matt begun writing about her? When had he started committing their private, personal moments to paper? Had those moments ever even been personal for him? Or had they simply been another "research" opportunity?

She'd believed he was filling her life with love and trust when all the time he'd been bleeding her dry . . . taking, using, betraying.

It had been difficult to endure what Gary had done to her, but she had come out of that painful episode stronger and wiser. She'd shored up her defenses and gone on, determined to keep herself from being hurt again.

But while her determination had made her cautious, it had not caused her to cut herself off from the world and its possibilities. She had recovered after Gary Beaumont. She was not certain she would be able to do that after Matt Michaels.

Oh, yes she'd be able to put her defenses back up again. But when she did, it would be forever. She'd wall herself away, lock herself up rather than risk being vulnerable again. Where suspicions and emotional caution had once merely shadowed her capacity to love and trust, they would now blot it out entirely.

Matt walked into the kitchen, his arms laden with brown paper grocery bags. His dark wavy hair had been trimmed to a somewhat more conventional length, but a lock of it still curved down onto his forehead. His cobalt-blue eyes glinted in their frame of black lashes. He deposited the groceries on the counter with a thud.

"Wait until you see what I have for you, sweetheart," he said, flashing his grin at her. With a conjurer's flourish he reached into one of the sacks and pulled out a huge bunch of daisies. They were wrapped in bright green tissue paper. He started to present them to Sara with another cheerfully theatrical gesture, then halted in mid-movement, his brows drawing together.

"Sara?" he asked sharply. "What's wrong?"

She didn't want to look at him, but he drew her eyes like a magnet. His closeness made her ache. "Gary used to give me flowers," she observed in a colorless little voice. "But they were always roses, not daisies."

"*Gary?*" He pronounced the name as if it were the vilest obscenity.

She nodded.

He put the flowers down on the table. "Sara," he said very carefully. "I am not Gary Beaumont."

She nodded again. Her features were utterly composed, but there was a bruised, haunted quality to the expression in her eyes. "I know that," she replied. "You're Mike Mathis."

"Mike—" He stopped abruptly, his eyes flickering down the length of the table. His entire manner changed when he saw the manuscript. At that moment Sara knew her worst fears must be true.

Gary Beaumont had blustered, bullied, and then threatened when she had confronted him with his deceptions. Matt did none of those things. Moving away from Sara, he picked up the stack of yellow papers. He rifled through the sheets once, his mouth twisting, then looked at Sara.

"So," he said in a strange voice. "You went through my things." He put the papers back down on the table.

She had expected such an accusation. Her father had blamed her mother for his infidelities and Gary had, in his manipulative fashion, tried to make her feel responsible for his actions. She lifted her chin slightly.

"Yes," she said baldly. She wasn't going to let herself get maneuvered onto the defensive and into an explanation about Chrissie.

He inhaled sharply, then expelled the breath slowly, a deeply disturbing glitter coming into his eyes. "You weren't supposed to read this."

"Obviously," she spat out sarcastically.

"This was something private."

She stood up, trembling like a leaf in a windstorm. *He* was the one in the wrong, not she! Yet he was doing his best to make her feel guilty!

"My life is something private, too," she told him rawly.

"I know that."

"You know that?" Her voice cracked with contemptuous disbelief. *"You know that?"*

She had to get away from him. Skirting the table, her vision partially clouded by a sudden welling up of hot, angry tears, Sara moved to leave the kitchen. Matt caught her roughly by the shoulders.

"Sara—" he began harshly.

"Don't touch me!"

"Then don't walk away from me!"

"I'll do whatever I want," she said in a low, furious tone, her gray-green eyes glassy with temper.

"Then I'll touch you all I damn please!" he exploded with something close to savagery. He shook her once, his eyes blazing with sapphire fire. "You just couldn't trust me, could you?"

"I trust—" No! She wasn't going to give him the satisfaction of knowing how thoroughly he had gulled her, how completely he had breached her defenses. "Why should I have trusted you?" she demanded. "From the very beginning, you held things back."

"And didn't you? Haven't you been holding back every single step of the way in this relationship?" he challenged her furiously. "My Lord, you've run the gamut from unfounded suspicions to something perilously close to paranoid delusions since I first met you."

"That's not true!" she denied, appalled by his words. True, she had suspected him of some things in the beginning, but not without good reason.

"Isn't it? God, Sara, I've tried with you. I've tried every way I could think of to help you feel secure. To tell you—to show you—" He let go of her so suddenly, she had to fight to keep her balance. "You aren't the only person in the world who's been hurt, you know. And you aren't the only one who's afraid to reach out because of it. But, dammit, Sara, you've let yourself get so caught up . . . so *trapped.*" He clenched his hands into fists, his jaw fretting as he struggled for control. "Do you have any idea what it's done to me, having you constantly doubt—"

She could not believe he was trying to do this to her, that he was trying to twist the situation around so the burden of guilt rested on her. "You're blaming me for what you've done."

Their voices clashed. His overrode hers. "You probe and test, question and push. You're always looking, searching, trying to find something . . . *anything* to justify this sense of betrayal you carry around."

She gasped. "I don't think *that* is just 'anything!'" she shot back, her voice vibrant with outrage as she pointed toward the manuscript. "When Tank Petrie said you told lies for a living, I thought he was making some kind of joke. But he didn't know the half of it! You've been *living* a lie!"

"You think what you and I—you think what I wrote about us was a lie?" He'd gone white.

"What you wrote . . . what you said . . ." She swallowed hard. She was not going to cry in front of him. She was *not!* "You told me you wouldn't hurt me."

"Sara—"

"You used me!" She threw the words at him, wanted to shatter him the way he had shattered her.

He stared at her silently for several agonizingly long seconds, his breath coming in deep, shuddery pants. His eyes were tearing into her. "Used you?" he repeated. "That's honestly what you think? You read what I wrote and you believe—"

"Yes!" It wasn't the full truth, but Sara didn't care. It didn't matter whether or not she had read everything he had written. She had heard enough from the two passages Chrissie had quoted aloud. "Yes," she repeated, "You . . . used . . . me." She spoke each word with poisonous precision. "You're welcome to cannibalize your own life, Mr. Mike Mathis, but stay away from mine!"

A graven image would have had more expression than Matt's face did when Sara finished speaking. Yet the stoniness of his strong features hinted not at a lack of feeling, but at powerful emotions held rigidly in check.

"So be it," he said quietly. The three words sounded

like a death knell. He pivoted on his heel and headed toward the door.

Sara was suddenly very frightened. "What are you going to do?" she blurted out in a choked voice.

Matt didn't even check his step. "Who the hell knows and who the hell cares?"

He didn't come back. Not that day, not that night, not the following morning.

Sara cried and cried, weeping tears she had suppressed for years. Her anger burned itself out, leaving behind the bitter ashes of betrayed love and a gnawing sense of loss.

Where was Matt? What was he doing? Who was he with?

Sara tried to tell herself she didn't care, but she knew that was a lie. The questions tormented her: The possible answers did even worse. She ached with a deep physical and emotional emptiness. The only thing she could fill it with was a soul-wrenching fear that she might never see Matt again.

During those first twenty-four hours alone she tried to occupy herself with mundane, mindless tasks. None of the endless series of chores she set for herself did much to dull the pain or silence the questions. The most any of them did was to get her through the day without screaming.

At midnight she crawled wearily into bed. When sleep finally overtook her, it was restless and filled with disturbing dreams. She woke up at five-thirty, shivering and desolate. She had never felt so alone in her life. Not after her father's desertion, not after Gary's betrayal— *never*.

There was no one she could turn to, no one to whom she could pour out her anguished confusion. Huddled up beneath the sheets, she confronted this reality without defenses. True, she had some family and a few friends, but there was no one to help take away the hurt that was ripping her apart.

No one except Matt. Yet how could that be, since he was the reason for her pain, wasn't he?

Of course he was! What was she thinking? How could she allow herself to have any doubts about it? Lord, in a few more moments she'd begin sounding like her mother. She'd find herself excusing ... overlooking ... accepting.

No! Sara was not going to do that. *She* was the one who had been wronged and she was going to hang on to her—

To her sense of betrayal?

Sara sat up, hugging her knees to her chest. Her eyes went wide against the darkness of the bedroom. She was acutely conscious of the hammer beat of her heart and the thrumming of blood in her ears.

How had Matt put it?

You probe and test, question and push. You're always looking, searching, trying to find something ... anything to justify this sense of betrayal you carry around.

But Matt had betrayed her, used her for his own ends, hadn't he? She knew what he had done, didn't she?

Finding these thoughts unbearable, Sara got up. Smudges of exhaustion shadowed the fine skin beneath her eyes and tiny signs of stress were etched into the set of her features. She showered and dressed, then wandered into the kitchen. The silence in the apartment, the feeling of emptiness, was oppressive.

One of the things she had done the day before was to unpack and put away the groceries Matt had purchased for their picnic. It had been a painful task. The assortment of pâtés and imported cheeses he had brought home recalled his sophisticated tastes and cosmopolitan style. The collection of delightfully decorated pastries reminded her of his imaginative and sometimes extravagantly whimsical sense of humor. A jar of her favorite extra-crunchy peanut butter set off a host of vivid memories of the man who had listened, learned, and loved with her.

Slowly, she got out the peanut butter and spread some of it on several pieces of bread. She had little appetite, but the gooey concoction gave her an odd feeling of comfort.

So did the casual little arrangement of daisies she had made in Matt's black lacquer vase. Sara stroked the glossy surface of the container gently, nibbling at her peanut butter and bread. She ruffled the white petals of the flowers lightly and stroked one or two of the sunshine-yellow centers. Her fingertips came away with a pale dusting of pollen.

Daisies. When she was a little girl, her mother had taught her a game she could play with daisies. He loves me, he loves me not, he loves me, he loves me not.

I love him . . . but I trust him not.

That was it in a nutshell—or was it? Again she found herself instinctively challenging a basic assumption. If she *hadn't* trusted Matt, why was she hurting so badly now?

That first night, when he'd come into the apartment, he had said he wouldn't hurt her and she had intuitively accepted this as true. It was only later that she began to conjure up the doubts and the questions. And that first time he'd wanted to make love with her, her body had welcomed him without reservations. It was only when she overruled her instincts that she had begun to resist.

She was the one she didn't trust! Because of her father and Gary, she constantly doubted her feelings and her judgments about people. Deep down inside she believed that she had been somehow at fault in both situations, and it had shattered her faith in herself.

Sara bit her lip so hard, she could taste the hot, coppery tang of her blood. Unbidden, her eyes moved to the manuscript that was still sitting, undisturbed, on top

of the butcher-block table. On the strength of two passages read aloud from those pages by somebody else,
she had rejected nearly two months of shared tenderness
and understanding as false. She'd told herself over and
over again that she wasn't going to let herself be hurt
again, yet on very flimsy evidence she had immediately
flung herself into the role of victim. She'd plunged the
knife into herself rather than let someone else have the
opportunity to do so first.

What if she had been wrong?

Sara took a step toward the manuscript.

What if she had been right?

Another step brought her to the kitchen table. She sat
down. After a long moment she leaned forward and picked
up the stack of papers. After another long moment she
began to read.

Chapter 10

WHAT SHE READ was not the draft of a new novel by Mike Mathis. It was a journal kept by Mathieson Michaels over the past three months. The pages were somewhat out of order when she first began, but she eventually shuffled them into sequence by using the dates written on each sheet.

The journal started with the last few weeks of Matt's cross-country drive—his "escape" as he termed it—from Hollywood. Matt saw himself at loose ends, traveling great distances but not really going anywhere. Sara winced when she read the way he took himself to task, using the same scalpel-sharp insight and cool detachment on his own failings and foibles that he brought to bear on the characters in his books.

The tone began to change with his arrival in New York. It was a subtle thing at first, but became more and more noticeable with each page. The emotions that surged across the sheets of paper were honest in their passion and their power.

"...I scared myself last night, and Sara, too," Matt had written the day after he'd come so close to making love to her. "But to finally touch her after so many days and nights of imagining what it would be like almost made me lose what little self-control I had left. And to have her pull back—God! Who did this to her? I could see the hurt and the memories in her eyes. What was worse, I could see her fear that I was going to hurt her, too. Maybe I'm a little afraid of that as well."

About ten pages later she found the erotic passage Chrissie had read aloud. Scanning the lines slowly, Sara realized that while she had heard the words as her sister had spoken them, she had been too caught up in her own tangled emotions to listen to their meaning.

"...I'm like a boy with his first girl with her," Matt had penned at the end of the entry, his words somehow communicating a sense of wondering, tender disbelief. "I feel like a new man—or maybe like the one I've always wanted to be. She makes everything seem fresh and right."

Sara closed her eyes for a moment, remembering her initial reaction after she and Matt had made love for the first time. *Reborn,* she had thought. *That's how I feel, reborn.* And Matt in some mystical fashion had shared that sense—as well as the intense physical pleasure.

Why hadn't he said anything? she asked herself.

Why hadn't she?

Trembling a little now, she continued reading. The trembling stilled in the space of a heartbeat when she came to the final passage:

"...Not too long ago, Tank Petrie asked me if I'd ever thought about settling down and having children of my own. Sara was there, and she turned her eyes away from me when he asked, so I made a joke about it. A joke! No one laughed, least of all me."

The last lines were scrawled across the bottom of the page in a dark, slashing hand. They read: "Sara, Sara, it's bad enough feeling you shut yourself in the way you do. But it's hell feeling you shut me out at the same time. I love you ... if only you could believe that."

Sara's vision blurred for a few moments and she had to blink hard to clear the sudden shimmer of tears that welled up in her eyes. She set the last page down on the top of the stack of papers.

"Oh, Matt," she said aloud, her voice barely rising above a whisper. "I love you, too. But how will you ever believe it after what I've done?"

She'd betrayed herself—and him—with her doubts. In her determination not to be blinded by love she'd made herself blind to it instead. And all the while she'd been defending herself against the possibility of being hurt, she'd given little thought to the pain she might be in-flicting on someone else by her actions.

No wonder Matt had reacted the way he did during the final exchanges of their quarrel! He believed she had read his confession of love and dismissed it as a lie. She had let him think—no, she had *told* him she wanted him out of her life.

And so he had gone.

"What are you going to do?" she had asked him.

"Who the hell knows and who the hell cares?" he had thrown back at her.

Sara cared ... and she felt a sudden and irrational surge of hope that there was someone who might know.

The lobby of the hotel was bustling with guests when Sara arrived there shortly before four. Fortunately for her, everyone was too caught up in his or her own con-cerns to pay any attention to a slender, mahogany-haired young woman wearing a tan trench coat on a day that had been distinguished by a cloudless sky and eighty-degree-plus temperatures.

Outwardly, Sara was quite calm: She even managed to give the doorman a pleasant smile as she passed by. Inwardly, she was tied up in emotional knots.

Pausing for a moment, her eyes swept around the lobby until she spotted a small, discreetly lettered sign reading HOUSE PHONES. Drawing her slim body up with determination, she headed in that direction, praying that no one would stop her.

Thank you, Lieutenant Santini, she thought.

She'd called him, using the number on the business card he'd given her. It had taken her a while to remember where she'd put it, but she'd finally uncovered it in a stack of bills and unread magazines. Her heart had been in her mouth as she'd dialed the police department number, and she'd steeled herself against the disappointment of learning that the lieutenant wasn't working on this holiday Sunday.

But, by some miracle, he'd been in and at his desk.

"Yeah, Santini," he'd growled into the receiver when he finally answered.

Sara had had to clear her throat. "Lieutenant Santini? This is—this is Sara Edwards. I don't know if you remember—"

"Sure I remember," he'd interrupted. "And I appreciate your giving Matt Michaels my message when he got back from out of town." There was a slightly sardonic edge to the remark.

"Oh." She'd winced. "I—I'm sorry I didn't tell you the truth, Lieutenant. But I thought—"

"Hey, hey, no problem. Matt explained. That's some imagination you've got, by the way. So, Miss Edwards, what can I do for you?"

She'd hesitated a long moment then explained, haltingly at first, but with increasing fluency as she went on, what had happened between her and Matt. Lieutenant Santini had punctuated her confession with little sounds of encouragement, letting her tell the story in her own fashion.

". . . so it's my fault," she'd concluded, her voice as bleak as her eyes. She twisted the phone cord around one finger.

"Whoa, now," Santini had said. "One of the many things I've learned in my time on the force is that almost nothing is 'all' anybody's fault. The blame should get spread around. Like with the misunderstanding about me being after Matt. Now, sure, you jumped to a wrong conclusion there and you were wrong for lying to me the way you did. But Matt was at fault for not telling you who he was—for not picking up on what you were thinking. And I don't win any prizes for the way I acted, either. So, I don't want to hear any more of this it's-all-my-fault stuff from you. Yeah, you've made a big mistake, but it takes two to make the kind of blow-up you just described." He'd paused, allowing time for his comments to sink in. "Okay. Matt walked out on you yesterday and you haven't had one word from him since."

Sara had leaned her head in one hand. "I—I don't know where he might have gone," she told him. "I thought . . . he said you'd gotten to know each other very well when he was researching *Tin Pigeon*—"

"Yeah, we did."

"I'm so afraid something may have happened to him!"

"If something had happened to him anywhere in this city, I would have picked up the squeal, believe me." Santini's tone had been firm and reassuring. "Now, knowing what I do about Matt, I'm willing to bet he's holed up someplace, pouring his guts out all over some damned yellow legal pad."

"I have to find him and tell him the truth. Do you have any idea—?"

"I've got a couple. Let me do a little unofficial missing-persons business, and I'll get back to you."

He'd called back about two hours later with the name of a midtown hotel and a room number. Sara had gripped the telephone so tightly, her knuckles had gone completely white. Her stammered words of gratitude had been gruffly brushed aside.

"Hey, I still owe him," Santini informed her. "Besides, I'm part-Sicilian, remember, and that means I believe in taking care of my own."

"But I'm not Sicilian . . . and neither is Matt."

"The way Matt cooks spaghetti sauce, he qualifies as an honorary Sicilian."

"You've had his spaghetti—?" Sara was feeling curiously lightheaded at this point.

"Who do you think taught him how to make it?"

They'd both laughed.

"Thank you, Lieutenant," Sara had said, suddenly eager to be on her way.

"It's Joe, Sara."

Thank you, Joe, she thought, picking up the house phone. She dialed the number to Matt's room with exquisite care.

One ring.

What if he wasn't there?

Two rings.

What if he was and he wouldn't listen to her?

Three rings.

What if he would and she couldn't find the right words?

Four rings.

She'd find them. She had to.

Five rings.

She had to because she loved him.

Six—

"Hello."

Sara sucked in her breath. It was Matt!

"Hello." His voice was taut.

"Matt . . . it's Sara."

There was a long silence on the other end. Her heart was pounding thunderously.

"Sara." He said it very softly, drawing it out. "How did you—?"

"Lieutenant Santini." Lord, she had so much she wanted to say! But not over the phone, not like this!

"Ah."

"Matt—"

"Where are you?"

"D-downstairs. In the lobby."

She thought she heard the ghost of a laugh. "In the lobby," he repeated almost wonderingly. "I was just going down there to check out when you—when the phone rang."

"To check out?" A wave of panicky despair swept over her.

"Yeah. I was going to go . . . home. Back to the apartment. Back to you."

"Oh, Matt," she could barely get his name out.

"Sara—"

"I want to come up," she forestalled him. "Please."

"The door's unlocked," was his response.

He was standing by the window on the far side of the room when Sara entered. Although his posture was perfectly relaxed, he was radiating an aura of tension. His face, although schooled into unreadability, held the same hints of strain and exhaustion she had seen the first night she had met him. Whatever else Matt had been doing since he'd left her, he had not been sleeping.

Sara shut the door. "I—uh—I b-bet you couldn't open this door with your credit card," she said, shifting awkwardly. The lock on the door was computerized and electronically operated.

"I bet I couldn't either," he agreed.

"You once said you'd teach me how to do it. Open

a door with a credit card, I mean." She was floundering.

Something stirred deep in his eyes. "Another promise I didn't keep?"

"No!" The word came rocketing out of her.

"No?" There was a challenge in the single syllable.

"No," she confirmed, meeting his gaze steadily. She moistened her lips. "Matt, I've been so wrong about so many things—what you said about my being trapped, about my trying to justify some sense of betrayal—" She gestured, struggling to put her emotions into words. "It wasn't you. It was never you. *I'm* the one I didn't trust."

His face was still terribly controlled, closed off. He was right. It *was* hell feeling shut out. "Is that why you went through my things?" he asked.

She shook her head once. "Chrissie was the one who found your manuscript."

"Chrissie?" His dark brows went up.

Lord, this was so hard! And he wasn't making it any easier. But why should he?

"Chrissie came by while you were out. She was on a stopover en route from L.A. to Italy. She just got a part in a movie that's being filmed over there. But she left her passport in the apartment when she went out to Hollywood.

"So she came by to get it," he finished. "Why did you let me think you had—"

"Because to explain to you would have been like defending myself! It would have been like *I* had done something wrong." She closed her eyes for a moment. She *had* done something wrong. Something dreadfully, unforgivably wrong. Steeling herself to continue, she opened her eyes again. "I told myself you were the one...the one who should have to explain and defend—"

"Because of what I wrote."

"I didn't read what you'd written until this morning."

"What?" The question was soft, barely a hiss of a

sound, but explosive in its emotionalism.

"Chrissie read two passages of it aloud to me when she found it. She read your description of me and of the first time we made love. Listening to it, I heard in some twisted kind of way what I needed to hear."

"You heard that I'd lied to you? That everything between us was—that I'd used you?" He'd gone very pale. His eyes were glittering with cobalt feverishness. "You needed to hear that?"

"No." She clenched her hands into fists, her fingernails digging painfully into her palms. She could feel the hot prick of tears welling up, threatening to fall. "When I finally read for myself what you wrote, I realized how wrong, how blind ... I read every single, honest word, Matt. But I shouldn't have had to. I should have known, have trusted myself and my feelings about you." She dropped her eyes to the floor as the tears began to spill over.

"Don't cry."

Not daring to look at him, Sara wiped her cheeks with one shaking hand. "I'm so sorry, Matt," she got out, and turned toward the door. There was desolation in the set of her slender shoulders.

"Then don't walk away from me!"

She froze. He'd said exactly the same thing to her in the kitchen the day before during their quarrel. He'd sounded angry then. There was a tormented quality to his voice now.

"Sara, please."

He'd closed most of the physical distance between them. She could feel his nearness with every fiber of her being and was filled with a wild mixture of longing and hope. As she turned slowly back to face him, Sara realized he was now standing close enough for her to simply reach out and touch. She wanted to do so desperately.

Instead, he touched her, using one gentle finger to follow the silvery trail of a tear as it rolled down the line of her pale cheek. He traced the curve of her lower lip with tender care, then withdrew his hand.

"I loved my father, Matt," she said, staring up into his eyes. "I loved him and he walked out on me and Chrissie and my mother. And I loved Gary Beaumont— or at least I thought I did—and he let me down, too. Then I met you and from the very beginning—" She managed a crooked smile. "You know that cliché about if it seems too good to be true, it probably is? Well, with my record I just couldn't let myself believe that I could finally be right about something as good as us." She took a deep breath. "I love you so mu—"

Matt cut the rest of her confession short by pulling her into his arms with a groan and bringing his mouth down on hers in a hot, hungry kiss. It was a devouring, demanding caress that sent her blood racing through her veins like fiery champagne and triggered an explosive response deep within her. With a soft whimper of passion she kissed him back, opening her lips to him in invitation. His arms closed around her possessively, but there was no need for him to press her against him. Her body was already fitted to his.

"I feel like I've been waiting my whole life to hear you say that, Sara," he murmured. "And I want to spend the rest of my life saying it back to you. I love you, darling. I love you."

The flames kindling within her were purifying ones, burning away the doubts she'd harbored for so long. "Oh, Matt," she sighed, her hands roving up his back, relishing the rippling play of his leanly muscled torso in answer to her stroking touch. "You don't have to say it."

"I'll say it," he returned, his voice growing thick as she reversed the route of her hands. He was undoing the buttons of her raincoat with more haste than dexterity. "And I'll show it. If I ever get you out of this damned rain—"

The garment parted abruptly and Sara heard Matt catch

his breath in surprise. Edging back a bit, she moistened her lips. Underneath the raincoat she was wearing nothing but the sheer batiste nightgown she had had on the first night they'd met.

"Where—" Matt had to clear his throat. "Where's your squash racquet?"

A soft flush mantled Sara's cheeks. She slipped the raincoat off, dropping it on the floor. It fell to the floor, a heap. "I knew I wasn't going to need it," she replied. letting her emotions show without shame or fear for the first time in a long time. She needed him . . . she wanted him . . . she loved him.

"Sara—"

"I know you said you don't usually do much revising of your work," she went on. "But I was hoping we might rewrite a few of our scenes together, correct my mistakes."

"Go back to the beginning?"

She nodded. Taking a step forward, she lifted her arms and put them around his neck. She was trembling a little, and so was he. "Something like that," she whispered.

He picked her up in a smooth movement, cradling her against him. She twined the fingers of one hand through the thick, dark hair at the nape of his neck. Her other hand went to the buttons down the front of his shirt.

"I've got a better idea," he said. "Let's make this our new beginning."

A radiant smile blossomed on her lips. "You're the author."

"And you, my dearest love, are all the inspiration— literary or otherwise—I am ever going to need."

It was like the first time for both of them, but with none of the awkwardness or insecurity found in initial encounters. Each touch, each caress, each whispered endearment, was fresh and new, yet erotically familiar.

They knew each other completely, yet they had so much to learn.

Trust made all the difference. Trust in each other and in themselves.

"You are so beautiful," Matt murmured heatedly against her skin, his tongue inscribing love poems on her quivering flesh. He kissed his way down her body, from her mouth to her taut, pink-tipped breasts, across the trembling plane of her fair-skinned stomach, adoring each part of her with an ardor that was as overwhelmingly passionate as it was infinitely tender.

She opened to him willingly, eagerly, not simply yielding to the force he was stirring within her, but giving and glorying in turn. She took all he wanted her to have, receiving it with unshadowed joy, then returning it with rapturous generosity.

She was greedy for his pleasure as well as hers—they were one and the same. The shuddering of his strong male body in response to the avidly intimate exploration of her lips and hands triggered a deeply sensuous answer in her own body. In arousing him, she aroused herself.

Sara was bolder, braver, and freer than she had ever been in her life. She molded and stroked the powerful breadth of his shoulders and chest and shaped the muscled length of his arms and legs like a wanton sculptress. She teased and tantalized, feasting on the flavor of him, feeling him gasp and go rigid with anticipation and expectation as her desires carried her further than she had ever gone with any man.

"Sara—" he groaned suddenly, the caressing flow of his hands over her body turning to a near-bruising grip. "I can't—let me—"

"No, let me," she breathed. Arching in urgent invitation, she allowed herself to be pulled up and against him. She felt the slick slide of skin over skin, heard the voluptuous rhythm of his heartbeat, knew the demanding quest of his manhood. "Let me . . ." she repeated.

He did. A moment later, their bodies merged in an act of ecstatic, mutual surrender. Perfectly balanced between giving and receiving, it was an act in which Sara took Matt as completely as he took her.

Afterward they slept. They awoke within seconds of each other, utterly refreshed, and shared a smile of deep, loving tenderness.

Propping himself up on one elbow, Matt gazed down at Sara with brilliant, crystalline-blue eyes. Reaching up, she touched his cheek in a gesture of gentle possessiveness, enjoying the faintly raspy texture of the beard growth she found there. She stroked the firm but soft flesh of his lips in turn. He responded by nipping teasingly at her fingers, his smile changing to that devilish freebooter's grin that had intrigued her from the very start.

"I love you," she said simply, her own gray-green eyes sparkling. "Ah . . . Matt!"

He'd begun walking his fingers slowly along the delicate line of her collarbone, balancing on it like some daring tightrope artist. The exquisitely sensual contact sent little shivers of pleasure scurrying along Sara's nerves. Her nipples tightened into yearning rosebuds and she gave a languorous sigh.

"And I love you," he replied with quiet intensity, bending his head to press a brief kiss on her lips. "Sara"— he paused—"I want to talk to you about what I wrote— what you read."

A tiny questioning line pleated the fine skin between Sara's brows, but there were no doubts, no apprehensions in her expression as she watched him. "All right," she agreed serenely.

"You were angry and hurt because you thought I was using you as research for one of Mike Mathis's books," he said evenly. "You were afraid I was going to cannibalize your life the way I've cannibalized mine."

"I was wrong to be afraid," she responded.

He shook his head. "No, you were right—in a way. I have used the people I know in my writing. Often I've seen them just as potential characters, their lives and their problems as pieces of some potential plot. Writing as Mike Mathis, I've been able to distance myself from life. I've been able to hide who I am and how I really feel." He paused, his eyes growing pensive. "Of course, things started to change when I was working on *Tin Pigeon*. Getting to know Tank and Joe Santini and some of the others—they became friends, not just research material. I think my experience with them had a lot to do with why I had to get out of Hollywood. I was fed up with pretend names, pretend people, pretend reality."

"There was nothing 'pretend' about what I read this morning," Sara told him softly. "What you wrote—"

"What I wrote I should have had the guts to say to you."

"Instead, you poured it out all over some damned yellow legal pad."

"What?"

She gave a rueful little smile. "When I called Lieutenant Santini—Joe—for help in finding you, he said that from what he knew of you, you were probably holed up somewhere, pouring your guts out all over some damned yellow legal pad."

"Hmmm, close enough. I've been scribbling on the hotel stationery." He stroked her reddish-brown curls for a few moments, obviously seeking the right words. "I started keeping a journal a long time ago, when I was a kid. It was a place to put down what I did, what I thought, what I felt. I wrote down all the things I couldn't—or wouldn't—tell anybody. It was supposed to be private, personal. One day, just shortly after my thirteenth birthday, my mother went through my room and found my journals. She said later she did it because she was concerned about my behavior, and, heaven knows, that concern was probably justified, given the way I acted during my adolescence. But, justified or not, she read what I'd written."

"Oh, Matt." He didn't need to say anything more. Sara understood. "And yesterday, when I reacted as I did—"

"It was like reliving a nightmare. Except that some of the things my mother read were full of a boy's anger and confusion, so her rejection of them was . . . human. But when I thought *you'd* rejected what I'd written—"

"Never again," Sara pledged fervently. "I promise."

"Ah, Sara."

They sealed their trust and their love with a slow, sensual kiss. His tongue delved ardently into the sweet interior of her mouth as she shifted herself, melting against his body in an enticing avowal of her seductive intentions.

"I hope someday you won't need your journals anymore," she told him as his mouth roved down the line of her slender throat. "I hope someday you'll want to tell me all the things you can't—or won't—tell anybody else."

"Someday is now, Sara," he said, lifting his head to look at her with searing sincerity.

His expression as well as his expert touch set off a delicious tremor of excitement within her. "It is?"

"Hmmm. Everything I've been writing for the past twenty-four hours has to do with you—with us."

"And?" she prompted breathlessly.

"And I've hit a writer's block that only you can break."

"H-how's that?"

"Well, to begin with, I've decided to start putting my own name on my books. I think Mathieson Michaels would look pretty good on a title page. But first, I want to see it on a marriage certificate, along with yours."

Sara went very still, her heart pounding with happiness. "You're asking me to marry you?"

He nodded. "I've never been married before, Sara.

Until I met you I never wanted to be. But now I'd like to try my hand at—er—doing a lot of very personal research on the story of two people who fall in love and spend the rest of their lives together. I've got the beginning...and the ending. It's the thirty or forty or fifty years in between I need your help with."

"Literary inspiration?"

"*Loving* inspiration."

"Will you dedicate this story to me?" Her eyes were glowing with a beautiful light.

"We'll dedicate it to each other. It's going to be a collaborative effort."

Her smile was like the dawning of a fresh new day. It was full of promise and trust. "Yes," she said with solemn simplicity. "As long as we can agree on the ending for this story of yours—ours."

Matt gathered her into his arms. "It's going to be a very happy one. Believe me."

And Sara did.

QUESTIONNAIRE

1. How do you rate _____
   ### (please print TITLE)
   - ☐ excellent   ☐ good
   - ☐ very good   ☐ fair   ☐ poor

2. How likely are you to purchase another book in this series?
   - ☐ definitely would purchase
   - ☐ probably would purchase
   - ☐ probably would not purchase
   - ☐ definitely would not purchase

3. How likely are you to purchase another book by this author?
   - ☐ definitely would purchase
   - ☐ probably would purchase
   - ☐ probably would not purchase
   - ☐ definitely would not purchase

4. How does this book compare to books in other contemporary romance lines?
   - ☐ much better
   - ☐ better
   - ☐ about the same
   - ☐ not as good
   - ☐ definitely not as good

5. Why did you buy this book? (Check as many as apply)
   - ☐ I have read other SECOND CHANCE AT LOVE romances
   - ☐ friend's recommendation
   - ☐ bookseller's recommendation
   - ☐ art on the front cover
   - ☐ description of the plot on the back cover
   - ☐ book review I read
   - ☐ other _____
     _____
     _____

(Continued...)

6. Please list your three favorite contemporary romance lines.
   _____
   _____

7. Please list your favorite authors of contemporary romance lines.
   _____
   _____
   _____
   _____
   _____
   _____

8. How many SECOND CHANCE AT LOVE romances have you read? _____

9. How many series romances like SECOND CHANCE AT LOVE do you <u>read</u> each month? _____

10. How many series romances like SECOND CHANCE AT LOVE do you <u>buy</u> each month? _____

11. Mind telling your age?
    ☐ under 18
    ☐ 18 to 30
    ☐ 31 to 45
    ☐ over 45

☐ Please check if you'd like to receive our <u>free</u> SECOND CHANCE AT LOVE Newsletter.

We hope you'll share your other ideas about romances with us on an additional sheet and attach it securely to this questionnaire.

• •

Fill in your name and address below:
Name _____
Street Address _____
City _____ State _____ Zip _____

Please return this questionnaire to:
  SECOND CHANCE AT LOVE
  The Berkley Publishing Group
  200 Madison Avenue, New York, New York 10016